CW01494897

A Cranberry for Christmas

By

Charlie Dean

Cover design by
Monica Dubinsky

For all the lovers of Christmas!

Chapter 1

'But he'll be there.' Alisha sat down heavily on the bed and stared at her friend's reflection in the mirror.

'And that's all the more reason why you should go.' Renee put her lipstick away and turned to face her. 'You must put on a brave face. It doesn't matter how much you're crying on the inside; you just smile and carry on. Never let them see that they've hurt you.'

'But they have hurt me,' Alisha whined.

'Come on, Alisha!' Lizzie called from the ensuite bathroom. 'It's been almost a year now; you have to face it sometime.'

'I don't want to face it,' she threw herself down on the bed. 'Can't I just pretend to be sick or something?'

'With some mysterious illness that hit you suddenly after everyone saw you at work less than an hour ago, perfectly happy and healthy?' Lizzie came into the room, towel drying her hair.

'Yes, I'll google one.' Alisha reached for her phone, but Renee was quicker.

'Shower! Now!' Alisha was about to argue, but the look on her two friends' faces made her get up and trudge sullenly into the bathroom.

'Meanies!' she shouted before closing the bathroom door and turning the shower on. She knew what they were saying was true. She'd avoided this situation at least ten times in the past year but she couldn't put it off any longer. 'Why should I be the one that loses out?' she asked herself as she stepped into the shower and started lathering up her hair. 'I've missed so many parties and things this year because of it.'

By the time she had washed and dried herself, she had a new attitude. Inside her stomach was churning but she was determined to go and show them all that Alisha Jones was back.

'Better?' Renee asked, seeing Alisha's determined expression.

'Much better.' She headed to her wardrobe. 'Time for this, I think.' She pulled out a long dress bag.

'Woah there, Nellie!' Lizzie stopped drying her hair. 'Not THAT dress.'

'Oh yes!' Alisha nodded. 'THAT dress.'

Renee looked at the pair of them with such a blank expression that Alisha and Lizzie just burst out laughing.

'I can't believe she doesn't remember.' Lizzie was gobsmacked.

'Well, perhaps if I could actually see the dress, then I might have some clue,' Renee said indignantly.

'That's what Alisha's dad said when he saw her in it.' Lizzie was now laughing so hard that tears were streaming down her cheeks. 'Thank goodness I haven't done my make-up yet.' She dabbed her eyes with a tissue and went back to straightening her hair. 'You tell her Lishe.'

'How long ago was it?'

Alisha dropped a hint. 'Christopher Knight's high school reunion?'

Renee's face lit up. 'You wanted to show Billy Davis what he'd missed out on by not taking you to prom,' Renee smiled.

'She showed everyone what they'd been missing out on,' Lizzie laughed again.

'Oh Alisha!' Renee's face went from smiling to a look of horror in an instant. 'No, you can't wear THAT dress.'

'Why not?' She unzipped the bag. 'I've got a good figure, why shouldn't I flaunt it?'

'I'm not saying you haven't but…' Renee paused. 'In something a little less revealing, maybe?'

'A bikini is less revealing than that dress.' Lizzie was now in absolute fits of laughter.

'You're not helping you know!' Renee scolded and Lizzie instantly tried to stop laughing, but the odd snort and giggle could still be heard. 'What about that lovely black cocktail dress you wore to Marie's engagement party? Or the blue fishtail number? The pink lacy one?'

She shook her head at each suggestion.

'Nope.' The bag was fully undone now. 'It's this one or nothing.' Alisha pulled out a slinky deep red dress with spaghetti straps, a plunging neckline, and a thigh high slit. It also had a deep back that just covered the wearer's bottom. 'Red is festive.'

'Oh dear God! It's worse than I remember! Well, on your head, be it.' Renee knew when she was beaten. 'But don't say I didn't warn you.'

'I'm so sorry guys,' Fay burst into the room, already half undressed. 'Arsehole boss kept me after work for two hours, then the bloody traffic was a nightmare.' Her clothes and shoes fell where she left them as she headed into the bathroom. 'What time is the limo coming?' She closed the bathroom door before re-opening it again seconds later. 'And to what do we owe the pleasure of The Billy Davis revenge dress?'

'Alisha's on a mission,' Lizzie replied.

'Yes, a mission to catch bloody pneumonia in that thing.' Renee shook her head. 'It's minus one outside and they've said it's going to snow later.'

'Well then I'd better find some gorgeous hunk of a man to keep me warm,' she wriggled into the dress. 'And I won't be needing these,' she threw off her pants.

'Dear Lord!' Renee looked to the heavens.

'That's the spirit!' Lizzie saluted her, and Fay just rolled her eyes before shutting the door again.

Less than an hour later, and all four girls were sipping champagne in the back of a silver limousine. They were now joined by Fay and Renee's other halves, Jimmy, and David, who were both in dark suits.

'Where is it this year, then?' Jimmy asked, his arm casually draped around Fay's shoulders.

'The conference centre,' Alisha replied. 'They were so good last year that Grandpa decided to go there again.'

'We went to a Halloween ball there the other year, it was amazing,' Lizzie recalled.

'Are these things really as good as you all say?' David, who was a recent addition, asked. He was a few years younger than them, and it was the first time he had met them all as a group.

'You just wait, David,' Lizzie patted him on the knee. 'You just wait.'

'Is your mum coming this year?' Fay asked.

'What the Christmas Grinch?' Alisha joked. 'Mum hasn't been to the Christmas ball since, err…never.'

'But it's her dad's factory.' Jimmy was confused. 'I know she's never worked there but why on earth doesn't she come to the balls?'

'She said she had enough of Christmas as a kid,' Alisha explained. 'Grandpa Frost…' There was a small giggle from Jimmy, which she ignored. 'Grandpa Frost started the business back in the sixties and he was hoping Mum and Uncle John would work there, when they were old enough, but only Uncle John wanted to.'

'And it's a Christmas factory, right?' David had picked up the odd bit of information from Renee. 'Called Frosts?' Jimmy giggled again.

'Yep,' Alisha nodded. 'We make everything from wrapping to tinsel and from baubles to crackers,' she beamed proudly. 'We're looking to diverse into the food side of it next year as well.'

'Ok Princess Christmas,' Lizzie teased. 'Leave something for the rest of the city to do.'

'We're meeting with a local business that's having money troubles next week to see if we can merge together somehow,' Renee rolled her eyes. 'Ok, no more business talk.'

'We have enough of it during the day, Alisha, at least give us the evening off.' Renee poured more champagne into her glass.

'So you all work there?' David looked around.

'Just me, Jimmy and obviously Alisha,' Renee replied. 'Fay wanted to be a lawyer and Lizzie here rebelled and went to work at Dunnings instead of Frosts.'

'Don't get me wrong, I love Christmas, but not all day, every day.' Lizzie remarked. 'The amount of glitter and tinsel that Mum and Dad bring into the house is unbelievable. I swear I have shiny shit sometimes because it must get in the food.'

'Dunnings?' They were all staring at David as if he'd just landed on a spaceship. 'I'm not from round here, I don't know.'

'There's two big factories in the city, Frosts and Dunnings. Dunnings makes clothes,' Jimmy explained. 'The majority of people around here work for one or the other and it's normally family and friends following on generation after generation.'

'Obviously I went to Frosts.' Alisha continued.

'Yeah, straight in at the top,' Lizzie complained. 'Joke, joke,' she immediately added following Alisha's gaze. 'Some people are so touchy.'

'We're here!' The limo came to a halt, and the driver got out to open the door for everyone.

'Oh Alisha, it looks fabulous!' But Alisha had turned deathly pale. 'What's the matter?'

'I can't!' She shrank and sunk back into the leather seats of the limo. Except for Renee and Lizzie, everyone else was now outside.

'Don't be daft.' Lizzie grabbed her arm and pulled it sharply. 'Come on!' One of the thin straps on Alisha's dress came down and her boobs almost spilled out.

'Who let me wear this dress?' She pulled the strap up hastily.

'I did warn you!' Renee was always right.

'Not now Renee!' Lizzie helped Alisha in readjusting her dress. 'You look amazing.'

'You really do Alisha.' Renee realised it was time to reassure rather than chastise. 'He's going to be absolutely gobsmacked when he sees you.'

'You never know, he might not even be here,' Lizzie said.

'Of course he will be.' Alisha tried to find some confidence inside. 'She'll be here, so he will be too.'

'I still can't believe they did what they did.' Renee shook her head. 'You just don't do that!'

'Are we going in or what?' Jimmy poked his head back in. 'I'm freezing my nuts off out here.'

'Alisha?' Renee and Lizzie looked at her.

'Oh bloody hell, come on then. I am Princess Christmas after all.' She took Jimmy's hand after Lizzie and Renee and arm in arm the six of them stood at the end of the red carpet.

'Wow!' David was awestruck. There was a huge snowman sculpted in ice by the entrance and a snow machine was blowing tiny flakes as they walked in. The walkway was adorned with red ribbons trimmed with gold and holly garlands, and two massive wooden Nutcracker figurines guarded the entrance inside.

They could already hear the music playing, but as they opened the glass doors, it became almost deafening. Inside, the room was alight with flickering candles. Golden candelabras adorned every table which were decorated in red and gold. Couples were already dancing on the snow-covered dance floor and Alisha knew at the other end was a winter wonderland complete with an antique carousel, roasted chestnuts, and stalls offering mulled wine and Christmas delicacies.

'There's Grandma and Grandpa.' Alisha pointed to the fabulously dressed couple waltzing around the floor. 'And Uncle John and Aunt Marcie.' She waved at the middle-aged couple seated at the top table.

'Your grandparents are so sweet, Alisha,' Renee sighed. 'Look at how he hugs her and how they stare into each other's eyes, as if they've just met.'

'They've been married fifty years next year,' Alisha commented. 'I hope I'm like them one day. They absolutely adore each other. It's the same with Uncle John. It must be in the male genes though, because my mum certainly isn't like it with Dad.' She hadn't realised that all the others except David were now staring behind her. 'Honestly, I'm surprised they're still together the way she talks to him sometimes.'

'What are we all staring at?' David asked, trying to work out what was going on.

Alisha saw their expressions and knew precisely what they were looking at. As she turned her head slightly her breath caught in her throat. He was right there!

Chapter 2

Despite herself, her heart melted at the sight of him. Her stomach flipped like a pancake on Shrove Tuesday and her knees felt like they had suddenly turned to jelly. Whether it was sheer coincidence or some inner voice telling him, he turned to look at Alisha at the exact same moment and his face broke into a big smile.

'Dear Lord, someone hold me up please.' Alisha grabbed hold of Lizzie in case her jelly legs decided to actually give way.

'Pull yourself together, girl,' Lizzie scolded. 'Just remember what he did.'

'Oh I know, but just look at him.' Alisha drank in the sight of him from head to toe. His dark blond hair was perfectly styled, his hazel eyes twinkling in the candlelight. He wore a dark blue suit and a crisp white shirt with a red tie and handkerchief peeking out of his breast pocket.

'No one is denying his gorgeousness,' Renee stated. 'But he's a prick!'

'Oh shit!' Alisha let go of Lizzie and stood up straight, smoothing her dress down. 'He's coming over.'

'Don't you dare be all smiles and nicey nicey Miss Jones,' Fay warned.

'I won't,' she promised and before she knew it, he was right behind her.

'Alisha.' He placed a hand around her back to draw her in closer to him so he could lean in and kiss her cheek.

'Jason.' She felt the warmth of his palm on the bare skin of her back, it lingered a little longer than was necessary and she found herself remembering the last time his hand had touched her bare skin.

She'd woken up on Christmas morning in her grandparents' house as she'd done every year since she could remember. The factory was always closed for Christmas and the entire family would arrive with armfuls of presents and food on Christmas Eve to spend the whole week together until the New Year. Even her mum couldn't fail to get involved and excited when the whole family was together although she still expressed a certain amount of 'Bah Humbug' at times.

Uncle John and Marcie came. They'd never had children and so doted on Alisha, her older sister and brother, Alison, and Alistair. Her mum and dad were there, of course, as were Alison and Alistair. Alison had recently split with her husband of two years, a fact which had dominated the majority of the talk so far. Alistair's fiancée Sally was coming later for dinner but for the first time ever Alisha had brought her boyfriend Jason.

Her grandparents were sticklers for tradition, so Jason had been assigned a guest room on the opposite side of the house to Alisha with strict instructions of no hanky panky before marriage. Alisha had blushed scarlet as they set down the rules in front of her and Jason, but he took it all seriously and promised her grandpa that he would be the perfect gentleman.

They'd only just taken their relationship to that level the previous month and it still felt so new and wonderful. But when Alisha had kissed him at her bedroom door, he had pulled himself out of her embrace, and with a cheeky wink, headed to his room.

It was early and by the silence that flowed through the house, it seemed that everyone was still asleep. There were no young children in the house anymore, so it was normally about 9 o' clock that people started to emerge from their rooms in their new matching Christmas pyjamas, which was a Frost family tradition.

Checking her phone, it was only half past six, so she decided to give Jason his Christmas present early. She put on the sexy red Santa dress she'd purchased from Ann Summers, along with black stockings that clipped into suspenders. She slipped on red velvet high heels, a Santa hat, and wrapped herself up in her very ordinary purple dressing gown.

Opening her door as quietly as she could, she peeked her head out. The house was still in darkness, all the bedroom doors closed. On tip toes she sneaked along the landing, avoiding the creaky floorboard she knew was outside her grandparent's room. She reached Jason's room without a hitch and stood outside his door composing herself for a few seconds before opening his door quietly and stepping in, closing it gently behind her.

It was pitch black inside, but her eyes had already adjusted to the darkness after being outside on the landing. She stared at the bed expecting him to be sleeping, but the cover seemed to be moving up and down. She cocked her head to one side as if it would give her a better view and realised that indeed the cover was moving up and down and there wasn't just one body in the bed, but two.

'What the actual fuck?' She turned on the lights and after squinting her eyes for a few seconds she took in the sight before her. She didn't know what she'd been expecting to see but it certainly wasn't this. Never in her wildest dreams could she have ever imagined this.

'Alisha, I can explain.' Jason was already reaching for his boxer shorts as she stormed out of the room slamming the door behind her. She didn't care who heard, didn't care if the whole house got woken up, all she cared about at that moment in time was ridding herself of the image that had burned itself into her brain.

Jason was behind her in seconds, his hair tousled and his face slightly red.

'What on earth's going on?' Grandpa Frost opened the door and switched on the landing light. He took in the scantily clad Alisha and almost naked Jason. 'What did I say to you?' he boomed angrily.

'Grandpa please, it's not like that.' It was only when he saw the tears running down her face did he realise that something wasn't right.

'Everything ok?' John and Marcie were at their door now, swiftly followed by Alisha's parents.

'Someone needs to tell me what exactly is going on here.' Grandpa Frost put his hands on his hips.

'Isn't it obvious?' Alisha ran to her sister as she opened the door. They'd always been close. 'They've had an argument, that's all.' She looked at Alisha as if warning her to agree.

'But why do we all have to hear about it?' Alisha's mum asked. 'I'm going back to bed.'

'Mother of the year again,' Alison whispered to Alisha.

'Is that what happened?' Grandpa Frost looked at Alisha and then at Jason, who both nodded. Alisha knew she couldn't tell her grandpa what she'd seen, not today anyway. 'Well then may I suggest that everyone gets back to bed for a bit and when we've all calmed down, we'll start Christmas again as it should be?' He turned to go back into his room before changing his mind and turning round again. 'And don't think this is the last of it. I want to know why you two went against my wishes.' And with that, he slammed the door.

Once everyone else was back in their rooms, Jason started to walk over to Alisha, but Alison put her hand up and shook her head.

'Not now!' she warned.

'But I just want to explain,' he pleaded.

'And you can, but not now, not today,' she said. 'In fact, it's probably best if you find some excuse to leave after breakfast. Actually don't wait till then, just go now.'

He bit back another retort but after a mumbled sorry to Alisha headed back to his room.

'Did you know?' Alisha hoped against hope that she didn't, but Alison nodded. 'Why didn't you tell me?'

'Oh, no sweet girl, I didn't know about that.' She kissed her on top of her head. 'He told me months and months ago, but I didn't realise, didn't even occur to me.' She pulled the dressing gown tighter around Alisha. 'If I'd have even suspected…well it would never have happened. Put it that way.'

'Do you think it's been going on for a long time?' she asked, allowing Alison to lead her back to her room.

'How could it have been?' she shrugged her shoulders. 'They only met yesterday.'

'I don't know whether that makes it better or worse?' Alisha sniffed.

'Try not to think about it for now.' She placed a hand on each shoulder and turned Alisha round to face her. 'Now be a brave little soldier, get yourself together and plaster a smile on your face.'

'I don't think I can?' Alisha looked down at the floor.

'Of course you can.' Alison cupped her chin with her hand and lifted her face. 'We are Joneses with Frost blood running through our veins and what do we do?'

'Never give up.' Alisha muttered the slogan that Alison had said to her on many occasions.

'I can't hear you?' Alison looked at her.

'Never give up!' she said it more forcefully this time even though she wasn't sure she felt it.

'Exactly!' she said as she pushed Alisha gently into the room. 'Now I'm going downstairs to get breakfast started and we're not going to mention Jason for the rest of the day.' Alisha nodded and shut the door.

'Is she ok?' Alison turned round to face the second body that had been in Jason's bed.

'Like you care?' she scolded.

'Thanks for not saying anything.' Alison stared in disbelief.

'I didn't do it for you, believe me.' She shook her head. 'I just didn't think Christmas morning was the best time for Mum and Dad to find out that you're gay.'

'Keep your voice down,' Alistair shushed. 'And anyway, I'm not gay, I'm bisexual.'

'I don't give a shit whether you're gay, bi or fucking omnisexual. All I care about is that you slept with your sister's boyfriend.'

Alisha, who had been listening behind the door, burst into tears, and flung herself onto the bed, pulled the cover over her head and hibernated until dinnertime.

Chapter 3

'Alisha!' The voice screeched in her ear and brought her right back to the present. 'We've missed you at the parties this year.' The tall blonde with legs up to her perfectly sized boobs bent slightly down to air kiss Alisha on both cheeks. 'Not ill today?'

'Marsha.' Alisha kissed the air back. 'No. Not ill today.' Alisha's eyes watched as Marsha snaked a beautifully tanned arm around Jason's waist and kissed him full on the lips.

'Jason darling,' she drooled. 'Let's find our table. I do hope we're on the main one like we should be. I couldn't believe the mix up at the summer soiree.' Her voice trailed off as they disappeared into the crowd of people heading for their seats.

'Who was that?' David asked, his gaze following the tightly toned buttocks in the skintight black dress and earning himself a thump from Renee.

'That was Marsha Underwood,' Alisha informed him. 'Executive assistant to my grandpa and Uncle John.'

'But likes to think she's above them both,' Jimmy piped in.

'And I presume the beefcake was Jason?' David had obviously been primed by Renee beforehand.

'In the flesh,' Alisha nodded.

'And they're together?' David asked again, to a nod from Alisha.

'Have been since she found out we'd split up after Christmas.' Alisha watched as the couple in question greeted her family and took seats at the top table.

'So…does Jason work at the factory then?' Alisha could see David was trying to work all this out.

'He's a sales rep from one of the suppliers,' Renee quipped in. 'Now are we going to dance or not?' She dragged him away without waiting for an answer.

'Come on, you!' Lizzie linked her arm through Alisha's and followed Fay and Jimmy to the tables.

'I don't care where Grandpa has put me, I'm not sitting next to Marsha and Jason,' Alisha whinged.

'Why shouldn't you sit at the top table?' Fay overheard and called back over her shoulder. 'You're Alisha Jones. Heir to the Frost fortune.'

'Joint heir!' She reminded her.

'Details!' Fay waved her hands as if Alison and Alistair were lowly peasants.

'There's Alison now with her new boyfriend, and look, Alistair has brought Sally,' Lizzie whispered. 'She looks amazing. Really got her figure back quickly, hasn't she?' Alisha had long ago forgiven her brother; she'd had to really. Sally had turned up for Christmas dinner later that fateful day and announced she was pregnant, so all talk had naturally turned to the excitement of a first grandchild and great grandchild, the new generation of Frosts even though this little one was of course a Jones. 'How old's little Danny now?'

'Six months.' Alisha doted on her little nephew. He was such a happy baby, always smiling, slept perfectly, drank his milk perfectly, in fact the only thing he hadn't done perfect in his short little life was being born on time. Sally's dates had been all over the place and in the end the little monkey had decided to arrive almost three weeks late despite Sally being induced a few times, little Danny Jones had refused to be born.

'Oh shit!' Lizzie had seen the table plan before Alisha. 'Why would your grandpa do that?'

'He thinks we're all best friends.' Alisha slipped in unnoticed with Jason on her right and Marsha on her left, giving Lizzie a thumbs up and a wry smile as she headed off to her own table before spending most of the meal as a gooseberry between the under the table footsie of Marsha and Jason and the leaning behind to kiss or stroke each other's arms.

'Well that was painful.' Alisha had moved off the table as early as was politely possible and joined her group of friends on the dance floor. She kept checking her watch, knowing that soon the outside doors would open, and they could all go out and enjoy the fairground stalls and rides.

'You should have just sat with us,' Fay stated, completely forgetting how things worked at the Frost factory.

'Ladies and gentlemen.' Her grandpa's voice came over the speakers as the last few notes of Kylie Minogue's Santa Baby died away. 'It's been another amazing year here at Frosts and we're looking forward to another fabulous twelve months with some exciting news on the horizon.' Everyone in the room cheered. 'I just want to thank you all once again for your hard work and MERRY CHRISTMAS!'

Balloons fell from the ceiling along with gold confetti, party poppers popped, and crackers cracked. The outside doors opened, and everyone cheered as the fairground music filtered in.

'I'm going to freeze my nipples off out here,' Lizzie scolded as they stepped outside.

'You are? Look what I'm wearing.' Again, Alisha regretted her decision to wear such a flimsy dress. It hadn't made her feel confident, all she'd done was worry about the straps, the slit and now she was bloody freezing.

'May I?' Alisha turned to find a tall, dark-haired man holding out his jacket for her to put on.

'You may,' she answered, slipping her arms into the jacket that was still warm from his body heat. It smelled slightly of aftershave, Jean Paul Gaultier if she wasn't mistaken, one of her favourites. 'Thank you…err?'

'Tom,' he smiled, his eyes twinkling and his hands sweeping down the sides of the jacket as if brushing away some imaginary fluff. 'Suits you.' She turned to face him fully. He was a few inches taller than her, with brown eyes and a slight stubbly beard. 'That dress is beautiful, by the way.' Alisha blushed at his scrutiny. 'But it would look much better on my bedroom floor,' he whispered in her ear. Even though she knew it was a line and not a very good one, she shivered.

'Come on, Tom!' Someone shouted and he waved at them before disappearing towards the dodgem cars.

'Santa Baby!' Fay had arrived after wrestling Jimmy's jacket from his shoulders. 'He can slip a sable under my tree any day.'

'I got Jeremy's again!' Lizzie was now wearing a brown jacket that was at least five sizes too big for her.

'Jeremy loves you,' Renee said, snuggling into David's jacket that they had somehow managed to both be wearing at the same time.

It was a tradition now at the Christmas party. It had started back in the seventies when there had always been a guest appearance by Santa and his reindeer outside of the venue. All the men had given their jackets to the ladies to wear, and it had been repeated ever since.

'I know and he's lovely, but I just can't think of him in that way,' Lizzie protested. 'Now this chap,' she indicated to Tom who was just getting into one of the dodgem cars. 'I can certainly think of him in that way.'

'I think he's already taken.' Renee waved a hand in front of Alisha's face.

'What?' Alisha finally stopped staring at him.

'Close your mouth, love, you're catching flies,' Jimmy joked. 'Who is he anyway?'

'No idea,' Alisha shrugged. 'Never seen him before, or the crowd he's with.'

'The one in the blue dodgem is rather tasty, too.' Lizzie's attention was suddenly drawn to a rather dashing looking young man with long blond hair. 'He's still got his coat on.' She shrugged out of Jeremy's, throwing it at Fay. 'Hold that, will you?' Fay caught it just before it hit the ground.

'Honestly!' Fay tucked the coat over her arm. 'That girl has no morals.' They all watched as Lizzie positioned herself at the exit to the dodgems and made a huge act of rubbing her arms and pretending to be cold.

'Well it worked!' David said. 'Look!' They all cheered as Lizzie arrived in her newly acquired coat.

'That's not all!' She waved her phone at them. 'Got his number too.' She turned and blew a kiss to the man who had recently been deprived of his jacket.

'Lucky heather.' A woman's voice called. 'Get your lucky heather.'

A middle-aged woman was weaving her way through the throng of people. She was dressed in a large sheepskin coat and a scarlet head scarf with tiny gold metal rings dangling from the edges.

'Has she seen us?' Fay ducked behind Alisha's back. 'Damn she's seen us, she's coming over.'

'What's the matter?' Alisha hissed. 'It's just a fairground lady selling heather. You don't have to buy it.'

'Of course you do,' Fay answered back. 'They curse you if you don't.'

'Don't be so ridiculous,' Alisha laughed.

'It's true Alisha,' Renee joined in. 'Don't you remember what happened to Janine Blackwater?'

'That was just chicken pox,' Alisha reminded them.

'Yes, we know,' Fay said. 'But who gets chicken pox on the morning of their wedding?'

'Lucky heather ladies?' She stopped in front of them, a wicker basket swinging from the crook of her arm.

'I'll buy some.' Fay was first in line, swiftly followed by Renee and Lizzie.

'And me,' Alisha stated after a nudge in the back from Fay.

'I apologise, dearie.' The lady rummaged through her basket. 'I'm completely sold out.'

'Never mind.' Alisha made to walk away, relieved in a way not to have to buy into the myth.

'I have this though.' She pressed a small muslin bag into her hands. 'Place this under your pillow just before you go to sleep on Christmas Eve and drink a cup of warm milk and honey. You will dream of your future husband,' she smiled a knowing smile, then walked away.

Chapter 4

'Why didn't I take his number?' Alisha groaned into her glass of red wine. 'Then I could be all loved up like you lot are, but instead I'm off to my grandparents' house for the traditional family Christmas as a singleton…again!'

'Because you're an idiot,' Lizzie soothed sarcastically. 'And you don't have the foresight to think ahead like me. I got Paul's number before I even got his name.'

The four girls were sitting in their local pub on Christmas Eve Eve. The place was crowded and noisy with work parties or people just having a pre-Christmas drink.

'He was just so lovely though,' Alisha whined again as her mind wandered back to the Christmas party.

It had been after one before the party had finally started to wind down. Most of the older revellers had long since departed but the younger Frost employees and their guests were still busy dancing the night away.

'And now, ladies and gentlemen, the last dance.' The DJ announced as the first bars of Have Yourself a Merry Little Christmas by Frank Sinatra started to play. All the couples blended into each other as Alisha stepped back from the dance floor.

'I'm so sorry.' She had bashed into someone and, after turning around looked up into the brown eyes of Tom.

'Shall we?' His voice was like silk as he offered her his hand and drew her into his arms. Her head rested comfortably on his shoulder, and she inhaled the smell of him. Definitely Jean Paul she said to herself as they shuffled slowly around the dance floor. It was so nice to be held in his arms. No demands, just two people enjoying each other's company.

The music had faded away along with Frank's beautiful voice. She'd looked up at Tom's face.

'Merry Christmas,' he whispered and brought his lips closer and closer to hers.

'Just one more then.' The DJ shouted and everyone started to jump around like mad things as Mariah Carey's All I Want for Christmas belted out. Someone had knocked into Alisha and Tom just as their lips had been about to touch.

'Sorry mate.' The man got straight back up to re-join his friends.

'Come on, Lishe!' Lizzie grabbed her arm and Fay grabbed Tom's before they had all started dancing and pointing to each other every time Mariah sang 'you'.

'That's it then folks.' The DJ had announced to many groans from the guests. 'All that's left for me to say is have a very Merry Christmas and a Happy New Year!'

The crowd cheered, clapped, and whistled before dispersing from the dance floor back to their tables to finish drinks and grab coats and bags. Alisha stood there dumbstruck like an awkward teenager, with Tom standing just as awkwardly in front of her.

'Well…I'd…' They both said together before laughing.

'I'd best find my friends,' he had said. 'I'm the designated driver tonight, so I'll probably need to round them up from under the tables.'

'Yeah, I should find my friends too,' she said, not knowing what else to say, desperately wanting him to stay but not knowing how to keep him there.

'I'll see you around then.' And that had been it, he was gone.

'Why so down Alisha?' Renee had asked, slightly drunk and leaning on David for support as they joined the others and picked up their various items that had been left lying around.

'I've still got his coat!' Alisha pulled his jacket from the back of her chair where she'd draped it after coming back in from the fair. 'Maybe I can catch him!' She ran, weaving her way through tables and slow-moving people before catching sight of him just outside by the door to the car park. 'Tom?' she called. He turned and smiled at her, urged his mates to go on ahead, and walked back towards her. 'Your coat?' She held it out for him.

'You keep it.' He took it from her hands and placed it round her shoulders. 'You've got more need of it than me tonight.'

'Are you sure?' She pulled it tighter around her body, hoping he wouldn't say no.

'I'm sure,' he smiled again. 'It's starting to snow.' She had followed his gaze outside the door where a few flakes were starting to fall and then had looked back at his face.

'Mistletoe.' She glimpsed the green leaf and white berries that her grandpa always hung above every door he could find.

'So it is.' But this time Tom wasn't taking any chances, he pulled her away from the door and the people that were leaving into a small corner. 'I've been wanting to do this all night.' He had kissed her then, softly, and slowly, pulling her into his arms as if he never wanted to let her go.

'Wahey!' The kiss had been broken by Tom being slapped heartily on the back.

'Give her one from me mate!' was the next bawdy retort.

'I'd best go.' He had allowed himself to be pulled into his group of mates that had obviously been lurking around.

'Earth to Alisha!' Fay's voice broke into her head. 'Honestly girl, you need to get a grip.'

'Sorry,' she shook her head. 'I'm poor company tonight.'

'Don't be silly,' Renee rubbed her arm.

'Yes, you bloody well are,' Lizzie agreed to looks from the other two. 'Well she is!'

'It's ok you lot,' she kissed the three of them. 'I've got to get home and packed anyway.' There were hugs all around and wishes of Merry Christmas and text you later. Alisha walked the few minutes to the taxi rank and hopped into a waiting black cab that took her home.

Unlocking the door, she kicked off her boots in the hallway and headed straight to the kitchen to make a cup of hot chocolate before going upstairs and into her room. Her small suitcase was already half packed and lay open on the bed. She picked some toiletries out of the bathroom, remembering to leave her toothbrush, toothpaste, and face wash for the morning and after removing her make-up, she threw the face wipes in as well.

After checking the weather app on her phone that told her lots of rain was on the way she went back down the stairs to fetch her rain mac that was hanging on the coat rack in the utility room. As she lifted it off its hook, she knocked a black jacket onto the floor. It caught her off guard for a few seconds before she realised it was Tom's and picked it up. It still smelt ever so slightly of his aftershave, and she cursed herself once again for failing to get his number. She didn't know his surname or where he worked, so couldn't even find him on Facebook. She'd already tried and there were far too many Toms on there to be clicking on every single one and who was to say his account was public or if he was even on there anyway.

An idea came to her suddenly, and she started delving in all the pockets. Maybe there was a business card in there, maybe he'd left his phone, anything that could help her find him. She knew she was clutching at straws, but she had to try. Her eyes lit up when she felt something, but her face fell when she realised it was just the muslin bag the fairground lady had given her. The rest of the pockets were empty.

Sighing, she trudged back upstairs and folded her rain mac neatly into the suitcase before hanging Tom's jacket up in her wardrobe. Would she ever see him again? She certainly hoped so. Surely, he was connected to Frosts somehow or he wouldn't have been there? They'd thought he'd been a friend of Lizzie's new beau Paul, but he hadn't a clue who Tom was and apart from asking everyone she could think of no one had heard of a tall, dark and handsome man called Tom at the party and if she didn't have his jacket to say otherwise, she'd have sworn she'd just imagined him.

The hot chocolate was just the right temperature, so she sat on her bed and drank it slowly, her mind drifting to what the next few days would have in store. She tried not to think back to last Christmas, that was dead and buried now. Jason had moved on with Marsha and Alistair was happy with Sally and the baby.

'Forget about it now,' she said to herself for probably the millionth time since it had happened. But it was hard. It didn't hurt anywhere near as much as it used to, but it was still slightly raw, especially when she thought about Jason. She'd fallen head over heels for him as she always did and thought he'd felt the same. She'd planned the wedding in her head and even practiced writing her name as Alisha Wright. She knew she was being silly, but she was only twenty-five and her mind was still that of a teenager sometimes.

She put her cup down on the bedside table and smiled wryly at the muslin bag that she'd put there.

'Stuff and nonsense,' she said, throwing it in the bin. 'As if sleeping with that under my pillow will make me see my future husband.'

She got her pyjamas on, moved the case from off her bed, and after reading for a while, snuggled down under the covers. Sleep eluded her, so she read some more and nodded off sitting up.

Her dreams were filled with a traveller woman, dressed in red dancing around a fire, her hips swaying hypnotically in time to a beating drum. She had bells on her fingers and toes, which chimed in perfect harmony with every step or sweep of her arms. She was smiling at Alisha, beckoning her to join in. There was a golden cup filled with a white liquid that she held out towards her.

'Drink this, my dearie,' she spoke softly. 'Drink this and dream.'

A thud awoke Alisha with a start and at first, she thought someone had been in her room till she realised her book had fallen on the floor. She switched off the light and pulled her duvet right over her head. It wasn't until the next morning that she realised the little muslin bag was now sitting on top of her clothes in the suitcase, not really knowing how it got there, she zipped up the case and took it with her to her grandparent's house.

Chapter 5

'Well, aren't you the rebel this year.' Lizzie greeted Alisha at the door of her parents' house and helped her in with her bags. 'I don't think we've ever spent a New Year with you.'

'I couldn't stay another day there, Lizzie.' Alisha hung her coat up on the hooks in the hallway. 'And Grandpa has only gone and invited Marsha and Jason for New Year's Eve.'

'She's really getting her feet under the table, isn't she?' Lizzie bashed Alisha's suitcase up the stairs. 'How long has she worked there now?'

'Eighteen months, I think, about the time I started seeing Jason.' Alisha followed her up the stairs, smiling at the family photos on the wall. 'Feels like forever.'

'Eighteen months, eh?' Lizzie opened the door to her bedroom. 'We've all known you how long? Yet still we've never had an invite to New Year at your grandparents' house.'

'I do try.' Alisha knew she was only teasing but still felt the need to explain. 'Grandpa says if I invited you lot, I'd have to invite the whole factory.'

'That's a cop out if ever I heard one.' Fay was sitting on Lizzie's bed. 'Renee is the only one that works for Frosts.'

'And why does bloody Marsha Underwood get an invite?' Renee came up behind them with a bottle of wine in one hand and a glass for Alisha in the other.

'Grandpa and Uncle John love her to bits,' Alisha explained. 'She's come in, turned everything upside down, implemented change after change, new systems, the lot. I honestly don't know where anything is anymore.'

'I thought she was just their secretary or something like that,' Fay stated. 'Aren't you meant to be the one that does all that?'

'I'm not experienced enough!' Alisha rolled her eyes and flumped down on a bean bag. 'Apparently having worked in the place since I was sixteen, having a business degree and being the owner's granddaughter doesn't count.'

'She came from Dunnings, didn't she?' Renee asked, and Lizzie nodded.

'Couldn't stand the bitch!' Lizzie took a huge sip of wine. 'Lording it over us like she was some big shot.' She took another sip. 'She went from trainee machine operator to business secretary in the blink of an eye.'

'Such a scandal,' Fay recalled.

'Only to those in the know.' Lizzie tapped a finger to her nose.

'Well I'm not in the know.' Alisha folded her arms in frustration. 'What haven't you told me?'

'It's just Chinese whispers, that's all.' Renee handed her a glass. 'You know what factories are like with their rumour mills? I've been going out with at least ten of the blokes off the shop floor if the rumours at our place are to be believed, three at the same time once.'

'But there's usually some truth in them.' Alisha blurted out, not realising what she was saying.

'Well thank you very much!' Renee laughed.

'You know what I mean,' Alisha laughed back. 'And how come you all know, and I don't?'

'She should know, really,' Fay said. 'After all, she's stuck with her now.'

'This goes no further,' Lizzie warned. 'Promise me, Alisha, it's for your information only, no blurting it out. I could lose my job.'

'Pinkie promise,' Alisha wiggled her little finger.

'I'm serious, Alisha.' Lizzie's voice was firm. 'I only know this because I was in the office when it all kicked off. If it ever got out the finger points straight at me.'

'Well now I'm really intrigued,' Alisha leant forward.

'I was with Mr Dunning Senior, going over the orders when all of a sudden Mrs Dunning Junior comes storming in and demands to see her 'adulterous husband and that trollop', her exact words.' Lizzie added off hand. 'Well, I don't know where to look. Poor Mr Dunning Senior is all flustered and lo and behold who walks in at that opportune moment but Marsha and Mr Dunning Junior from lunch.'

'No!' Alisha's mock gasp was ignored by Lizzie.

'I know it's not unusual to have lunch with your boss, but this happened every day plus they worked late every evening.' She made quotation marks with her fingers at 'worked late'. He'd been disappearing at weekends, not answering his phone, and giving false alibis to where he'd been.'

'I presume they were having an affair, then?' Alisha knew this was the way the story was going.

'Got it in one,' Lizzie nodded. 'The little tart had slept her way to the top. I think she was after Mr Dunning Senior, if you ask me, but Junior had to do.'

'It's women like her that give us a bad name,' Renee seethed. 'Why can't they just work hard like everyone else has to?'

'Still doesn't explain how she got the job at our place though,' Alisha commented. 'I mean, if up until then she'd just been a machine operator, then how does she have the experience and knowledge to do what she does now?'

'She's definitely got the experience,' Lizzie said, and Alisha knew she was being sarcastic. 'And Dunning gave her such a glowing reference that she could have walked into any job.'

'Well why did she have to walk into mine?' Alisha sulked.

'At least you don't get it in the neck from her all the time like I do?' Renee moaned. 'The way she waltzes round the factory inspecting every little thing.'

'Bloody hell you two, perk up, will you?' Fay pulled a bottle of vodka out of her bag. 'I won this at the work's Christmas party. It's cinnamon flavoured with little flecks of gold in it.' She tipped the bottle up, and they watched the gold float around like a snow globe.

'Very festive,' Renee said before turning her attention to Alisha. 'Speaking of Christmas parties…'

'What?' Alisha looked at the three faces that were suddenly focused on her.

'You know what!' Renee teased.

'I bloody well don't.' She looked at them with a blank expression.

'The fairground lady…' Lizzie suggested. 'The little potion thing she gave you…'

'Oh that.' Alisha waved her hand flippantly. 'I threw it away.'

'No you didn't.' Fay accused. 'You can't lie to us young lady.'

'Look she's gone red,' Lizzie pointed. 'You did it didn't you?'

'Come on, spill the beans.' Renee said eagerly. 'Julie did a similar thing with some wedding cake once and she dreamt of this chap Tim she knew from school. Only ended up marrying him a few years later.'

'Well I dreamt of a cranberry,' Alisha said moodily, taking a large glug of wine.

'I knew you'd do it,' Fay laughed. 'But a cranberry?' she laughed again.

'And in what context was the cranberry…exactly?' Lizzie was trying to keep a straight face but failed miserably when Fay and Renee burst into laughter.

'Stop laughing you lot.' She hit Renee, who happened to be nearest with a pillow. 'I knew it wouldn't work.'

'Tell us the full dream,' Fay suggested. 'Maybe you're missing something.'

'Yeah, go on, tell us the whole dream,' Lizzie agreed. 'Maybe there's a turkey in there too.' This caused the three of them to fall on the floor in fits of laughter. Alisha glaring at them over her glass.

'I'm not telling you if you're going to laugh,' Alisha huffed.

'We're sorry.' Fay was the first to recover and picked herself up off the floor, tears rolling down her cheeks. 'It's just…a cranberry!' The laughter began again and the more they tried to stop, the more they laughed.

'Are we finished now?' Alisha asked after nearly ten minutes of laughter, comments and innuendo.

'You have our undivided attention and promises of no more laughter.' The three of them had finally composed themselves and were now sitting cross legged on the floor in front of Alisha like school children waiting for the teacher to tell them a story.

'It's really not that big of a deal,' Alisha shrugged.

'Just tell us.' The three of them screamed at her.

'Ok then.' She held her hands up in surrender. 'I did exactly what the lady told me to do, and I dreamt it was Christmas morning, but I wasn't at Grandma and Grandpa's home. I was all on my own at my house, cooking Christmas dinner. A teeny-weeny little turkey crown in the oven.'

'Just like that Christmas Wrappin' song by The Waitresses,' Fay butted in. 'You know the one…world's smallest turkey.'

'Oh, I love that song,' Lizzie piped in and began singing.

'Ah hum,' Alisha coughed.

'Sorry,' Lizzie looked downcast at the floor. 'Do go on.'

'So, then it flashes forward to me sitting down at the table, still all on my own. Dinner all steaming hot on the plate.' Alisha paused for a second in case anyone was going to interrupt again but the three faces were eagerly awaiting the next part of the story. 'I reach for the jar of cranberry sauce…'

'But you don't even like cranberry sauce?' Renee piped in. 'You don't like any sauces except mayonnaise and even then, only…ok, I'll shut up,' she said sheepishly after a withering look from Alisha.

'So, I open the jar and instead of it being full of thick red sauce there's literally just a single cranberry in there.'

'Nothing else?' Lizzie asked.

'Not a thing.' Alisha shook her head. 'The jar is immaculately clean with just a single solitary cranberry at the bottom of it. But it's all shiny and sparkly like it's been out in a frost and instead of the green stalk it's got a Christmas bow on the top.'

'It's a very strange dream,' Fay commented.

'I haven't finished yet.' Fay whispered 'sorry' as Alisha continued. 'I dip a fork into the jar but each time I try and prick it, I miss so I tip the cranberry on to my plate from which all the food has now magically disappeared. As soon as it comes out of the jar it starts getting bigger and bigger until it bursts, but when I look down on the plate there's a wedding ring.'

'Well isn't it obvious?' They all looked at Renee, gobsmacked.

'Please enlighten us,' Alisha said. 'I've been pondering it for a week now and can't come up with a single sensible explanation.'

'You're going to meet someone or have already met them but you're not going to marry them till they've got really, really fat.' She fell on the floor laughing again, swiftly followed by the other two.

'I said sensible.' Alisha hit her again with a pillow to which Renee retaliated and within seconds the four of them were screaming and slapping each other with pillows, cushions or whatever else they could get their hands on.

Chapter 6

Three days later and Alisha groaned as her alarm clock rang shrilly at six in the morning. She slammed the snooze button and turned over, pulling her duvet up over her head. The alarm went off, and she pressed snooze a further four times before eventually dragging herself into the bathroom, dodging the used tissues she'd thrown out in the night. It was always the same every year, as soon as all the build-up and stress of Christmas and New Year was over, she got a cold.

It had started even earlier this year. She'd woken up at Lizzie's with an horrendous hangover on New Year's Day and after the rest of the day in bed had awoken the following morning back at home with a pounding headache and a bunged-up nose.

She was still half asleep as she stepped into the shower, then screamed and jumped out as ice cold jets hit her face.

'What the hell?' she tentatively tested the water, but it wasn't getting any warmer, so she switched it off. 'Great!' She touched the radiator in her room, this was also freezing. 'Looks like greasy hair and two days in bed sweat for the first day back at work. Thank goodness it's only family I have to see today.'

Hurriedly rubbing herself dry, she wrapped her dressing gown around her and slipped into fluffy slippers before heading downstairs to grab her shirts out of the washer/dryer.

'Oh, for fuck's sake!' She pulled five soaking wet blouses and three skirts out of the machine realising that she hadn't put it on the right setting, and they had completely missed the spin cycle and instead of being lovely and warm were just absolutely dripping wet and would take hours to dry. 'That's what you get Alisha Jones for leaving it to the last minute, as usual.' She switched the kettle on and picked up her phone while she waited for it to boil, only to find she hadn't switched that on to charge last night either and it was flat as a pancake.

Twenty minutes, a strong cup of coffee and two slices of toast later, she was feeling slightly more with it. Quickly washing her face in cold water, she stood in front of her wardrobe, agonising over what to wear. Her usual work attire was currently lying in a sodden heap on the kitchen floor, so she squeezed into a pair of black trousers that she hadn't worn for over a year and cursed the extra half a stone she'd put on over Christmas.

The top button wouldn't quite reach over her bloated stomach, so she knew she had to wear a longer top, especially as she was now also suffering from the most in your face visible panty line going. Reaching for the smartest thing she could find in her wardrobe; she pulled on a black jumper and dressed it up with some jewellery.

Staring at herself in the mirror, she twisted her hair into a bun, despaired at what she looked like and then ran down the stairs when she realised that she should have been at work half an hour ago. Grabbing her keys, she unlocked the door, screamed at the thick frost that was covering her car before frantically scraping the ice with her credit card when she remembered she'd forgotten to buy a new scraper for the winter.

She was nearly three quarters of an hour late when she actually got off her drive and took the usual route to work, forgetting that the road was closed off for the following three weeks to fix a major water leak that had caused Plough Hill Road to be nicknamed by the locals as plough me a river.

Swearing and doing a rather ungraceful nine-point turn, she followed the diversion signs which added an extra five miles to the journey and finally pulled up in the factory car park over an hour later than she should have been. She ran up the four flights of stairs that took her to the top offices that looked out onto the shop floor, catching her jumper on one of the door handles as she sped past to reach her grandpa's office.

'What else can go wrong today?' she asked as she unhooked herself and realised that the jumper now had a massive tear down one side. 'I am so sorry, Grandpa.' She opened the door and rushed in, pulling her bag over her head, and catching her jumper again but this time on the buckle of the strap. 'Been an absolute nightmare,' she said as she tried to extradite herself from her bag and jumper which had somehow managed to go over her head. 'My water and heating aren't working and then the washing machine broke.' She didn't think her grandpa would appreciate her forgetfulness and thought this may invoke some sympathy towards her predicament. 'The car was covered in ice, and they've closed the road off, so I had to go the long way round and to top it all off I've got a stinking cold and a nose to rival Rudolph the red nosed bloody reindeer.' The last words were spoken as she finally freed herself and smoothed down her jumper. 'Oh...hello everyone.' She blushed furiously as she realised her grandpa was not alone in the room, in fact, he was far from alone. Sitting in front of the desk was Uncle John, Alison, Alistair, Marsha, some older man Alisha didn't know and dear God, no it couldn't be, anyone but him.

'Lovely to see you again, Alisha,' Tom smiled at her and winked.

'We were just chatting about the merger.' Her grandpa gave her a stony look and she knew she'd be for it later. 'This is Mr Walker.' He indicated to the middle-aged man sat next to Tom and Alisha shook his hand. 'And his son Tom who I presume you met at the party?'

'Tom very kindly leant me his jacket.' Alisha said as she sat in the only empty chair that was placed rather inconveniently right next to Tom.

'Shame you didn't borrow it again today.' Marsha sniped quietly, but loud enough so everyone in the room could hear, and Alisha shot her a withering look while Alison and Alistair giggled.

'Nothing wrong with casual attire,' Mr Walker said, and Alisha instantly warmed to him. 'I hate having to wear stiff shirts and tight ties all the time.' And with this, he undid his tie and unbuttoned his shirt collar.

Grandpa Frost, who was never seen without a full suit on except in the summer when he dispensed with his jacket and wore a waistcoat instead, was a little taken aback but hid it well and continued talking. Alisha who had presumably missed a good chunk of the meeting as she could tell her grandpa was in his closing phase, stared out of the window and tried not to think about Tom's knee that was now touching hers.

She couldn't move it, that would just be rude and anyway she didn't want to move it even though she could feel the heat from his body passing into hers, pulsing through her thigh and up into...

'Alisha!' Her grandpa's voice interrupted her thoughts, and she saw Alison and Alistair look down and hide smirks behind their hands.

'Yes, Grandpa,' she answered, not knowing what she was actually saying yes to.

'The cash flow projection?' He was staring at her now and his usual calm face was starting to redden. 'Have you got the figures, child?'

'I think...' She rifled through her bag. 'I put them...' More searching. 'They should be...'

'I've got a copy in my office, Mr Frost.' Marsha stood up and Alisha knew she'd lost what little credibility she may have been able to salvage from this meeting. As usual, she was dressed impeccably in a short-tailored dress that hugged every curve, her hair freshly washed, and make-up perfectly applied. 'If you would just give me five minutes, I'll pop downstairs and run a few copies off for everyone.'

'Thank you, Marsha,' Grandpa Frost almost simpered at her before turning to Alisha. 'I think we could all do with a cup of tea while we wait.'

'Yes Grandpa,' she stood up.

'Actually, I'll have an espresso please, Alisha.' Marsha was already halfway out of the door before she turned. 'And Mr Walker takes his tea white with two sugars and Tom has his coffee like me, hot and strong.' Alisha's mouth dropped open, and Alison and Alistair had almost slipped out of their chairs as they tried not to laugh, even Uncle John was having a hard time keeping a straight face.

'I think I'll have tea today,' Tom said before standing up. 'And I'll give you a hand to make them.' Alisha wished she'd had a camera at that very moment. The look on Marsha's face was a picture, but it vanished as quickly as it had appeared, and she disappeared out of the door and down the stairs, her heels clicking angrily with every step.

'You really didn't need to help me,' Alisha said as she pressed the button on the drinks machine for the third time.

'I thought you needed rescuing.' He was leaning against the counter, his arms braced behind him, his hands resting on the work top. He was dressed smartly in a grey waistcoat, grey trousers, and pristine white shirt, but had clearly dispensed with his jacket a while ago as Alisha remembered seeing it slung on the back of his chair. He didn't wear a tie; in fact, his shirt had a more casual collar and was open slightly. Alisha fought back the urge to undo it further and see what lay underneath.

'I can handle Marsha.' She switched the cups again, mentally working out that after the next one she was going to have to reach above him for more drink pods. 'She likes to think she knows everything.'

'Yes, I got that impression when I first met her. Why does your grandfather take her everywhere? I'm sure Dad said yours was a family run business, that's why he's considering the merger. But she was never introduced as his granddaughter. Is she his great niece or something?'

'No, she's just a little trollop that slept her way to the top, got found out and is now trying to wheedle her way into my family.' Alisha thought twice before saying this and, in the end, decided to go with a much shorter version. 'No, she isn't family.'

'And anyway, I didn't mean Marsha. I'm sure a savvy girl like you can handle someone like her.' He looked her straight in the eye. 'I meant your grandfather, he's a bit of a dragon, isn't he?'

'He's a bit over the top sometimes.' The machine dribbled out the last of the tea. 'It's only because he wants us to be the best we can be.' She picked up the full cup, knowing that now she had to either reach behind him to get the coffee pods out or ask him to move and have him squeeze past her in the overly small confines of the kitchen. 'Can I just...?' She decided on the former and stretched her arm out towards the door handle just above his head.

'Here, let me.' His hand brushed hers as he turned and reached up. Electricity shot up her arm and she had to stop herself from pulling it away in case he thought she was recoiling from him, when in fact it was the very opposite. 'These ones?' He handed her a box obviously oblivious to the fact that his mere touch caused her to burn and ache for more.

'They're the ones,' she nodded, her voice cracking slightly. 'And I need two of those as well for Marsha and Uncle John.' She went towards the espresso pods at the same time as him and instead of grabbing them, she grabbed his hand instead. 'Oh sorry,' she laughed nervously, but didn't let go of his hand.

He was so close to her now that she could see the pulse throbbing in his neck, and she longed to press a soft kiss upon it. He tilted his head slightly to look at her, their hands still touching, in fact they were now intertwined. Slowly, painfully slowly, their heads moved towards each other. Alisha bit her lip in anticipation, all thoughts except that he was going to kiss her had left her head. She could feel his warm breath on her lips now, agonisingly millimetres away.

'Grandpa sent me to see what was taking you so long.' Alisha and Tom shot apart like guilty teenagers being caught snogging behind the bike sheds at the sound of Alistair's voice coming down the stairs.

'Nearly done.' Alisha handed him two cups. 'Take these up and we'll bring the rest.'

'Ready to go back up, Tom?' Marsha was now standing at the door, a neat pile of perfectly stapled papers in her arms.

'Here's your tea and one for your father.' Alisha handed him two mugs.

'I should have remembered,' Marsha laughed knowingly. 'You always drink tea in the mornings.'

Chapter 7

Alisha was still experiencing the humiliation of being demoted to the lowly job of tea girl even after the meeting had ended. Using a suspiciously pre-prepared power point presentation that Alisha had no part in, Marsha had brilliantly managed to take over the meeting's financial portion on her own. The printed copies she distributed also bore little relation to what Alisha had been working on at all.

But even as she delved further and further into her thoughts about the meeting and sank deeper and deeper into depression, one thing rolled over and over in her mind.

'I should have remembered; you always drink tea in the mornings.' Marsha's comment insinuated prior and possibly intimate knowledge of Tom's morning routine. Had they been in a relationship? A one-night stand, perhaps? Since Tom had only hinted that he knew her, it was unclear how he did.

'Daydreaming again, little sister?' Alistair asked as he entered the office that he shared with her and Alison.

'I can't get this blasted bank to reconcile again.' She threw down the red pen she'd been using to check each of the month's transactions from the bank statement to the computerised accounts. 'Four times I've tried now and I'm out by different amounts each time. I never had this problem with Sage.'

'Just put it to one side and try again tomorrow,' he suggested, pulling out his high-backed leather chair and sliding into it as if it was a piece of heaven. 'I just love these new chairs Marsha got us all for Christmas. All personalised to our seating position and everything.'

'I wouldn't know.' Alisha shifted uncomfortably on the bar stool she'd been forced to borrow from the factory floor after all the old office chairs had been given to charity on the last day of work before Christmas, with shiny new ones arriving to replace them all just moments later. It had only been that morning that they'd realised Alisha's hadn't been delivered.

'It's a shame yours didn't come.' He twirled round as if to show off.

'Isn't it?' Alisha was pretty sure it hadn't even been ordered because apparently the chair was now no longer available, but Marsha had assured her she would purchase something equally as fabulous. Alisha, however, wasn't holding her breath and made a mental note to visit Argos on her way home and pick up a new chair for herself.

'So…' Alistair tapped away on his keyboard. 'You and Tom…'

'What do you mean?' Alisha shoved the bank statements into a drawer angrily and closed down the accounts on the computer. 'Me and Tom? There is no me and Tom.'

'Pull the other one,' he said, grinning.

'Seriously,' she exclaimed. 'We've kissed once.'

'I knew it.' He leaned forward in his chair to face her. 'Spill.'

'It was just a Christmas kiss under the mistletoe.' She waved her arms as if it had meant nothing, yet it had meant everything. 'I never thought I'd see him again. I didn't know he was Mr Walker's son. I didn't even get his phone number.'

'Oh, he doesn't have a phone,' Alistair went back to his tapping.

'Beg pardon?' Alisha, who had just been about to start working on the time sheets, popped her head out to the side of her monitor to stare open mouthed at her brother.

'He doesn't have a phone,' Alistair stated again. 'None of them do.'

'They don't have phones,' Alisha repeated. 'How can they not have phones?'

'Some religion thing,' he said offhand. 'No social media, internet that sort of stuff.'

'You are joking, right?' He had to be joking, everyone had phones these days.

'Don't you remember the Deaton family at school?' Alison had just walked in to catch the tail end of the conversation. 'There was one in virtually every year. Angus was in mine, you had Joshua and I think Victoria was in Alistair's.'

'I remember,' Alisha answered. 'They used to have to go out of the room every time the TV was wheeled in.'

'Wouldn't it be bliss to live without technology?' Alison sighed as she switched on her computer to numerous beeps, announcing the presence of unread emails. 'Most of these are utter rubbish.'

'No Facebook? No Twitter?' Alisha was horrified. 'How can you live like that?'

'Quite easily,' Alison pulled out her phone. 'Not one social media app on here.'

'Since when?' Alistair, who was nearest, grabbed her phone. 'Where have they all gone?'

'Deleted and deactivated.' She took her phone back. 'I was spending so much time looking at other people's lives that I was forgetting to live my own.' Alisha and Alistair stared at her dumbfounded. 'I've joined a yoga class; go swimming and next week I'm enrolling on an evening art course.'

'Who are you and what have you done with our sister?' Alisha, who knew Alison was as bad as her for social media, wasn't convinced.

'Honestly, you should try it.' She started tapping away on the computer, answering her emails. 'Great for the sex life too,' she winked.

'Chance would be a fine thing,' Alisha tutted. 'Not a sniff of a boyfriend since…' she trailed off and Jason's name was left hanging in the air.

'What about Tom?' Alison changed the subject as quickly as she could.

'He probably doesn't believe in sex before marriage, either.' Alistair laughed nervously, grateful that the conversation had moved away from previous boyfriends.

'That would just be my luck.' She rested her head on her hands. 'I can't even contact him, can I?'

'You can send a fax,' Alison replied. 'They collect them from the local shop.'

'As if I'm going to do that?' Alisha scoffed. 'Imagine the shop keeper reading it.'

'Dear Tom.' Alistair put on a mock female accent. 'Would you like to meet me for dinner and possible pre-marital sex?' He ducked as Alisha threw a pen across the room. 'What was that for?'

'I wish I could just fly away from all this crap.' Alisha grabbed another pen out of her desk top tidy and angrily ticked off hours against the log.

'One day I'll fly away…' Alison began a rendition of the Randy Crawford song that had had a recent revival due to the John Lewis Christmas advert. She ducked as Alisha threw another pen. 'What's got your knickers in a twist?'

'I'm just fed up!' Alisha threw her hands in the air. 'It's alright for you two. You're the eldest.' She pointed at Alison. 'And you're the boy.' She pointed to Alistair. 'I get all the shitty jobs, you get to liaise with clients, have board meetings and what do I get? I get to make the bloody tea.' She went to slump back in her chair, then remembered it was a stool and ungracefully ended up in a heap on the floor. 'For fuck's sake.'

'Your grandfather wants to see you all in his office.' Marsha popped her head round the door. 'New yoga pose Alisha?' She sneered before closing the door again.

'New yoga pose, Alisha,' she mimicked. 'I'll give her new yoga pose and shove it up her arse.'

'You need to calm down,' Alison said with Alistair nodding in agreement.

'She does my bloody head in.' Alisha stood up. 'Swanning round like she owns the place.'

'Why are you so down on her all the time?' Alistair asked. 'She's only doing her job.'

'You are hard on her, Alisha,' Alison concurred. 'You always have been.'

'I just don't like her.' She led the way through the door with her brother and sister behind, tempted to inform them of the information she had discovered about Marsha over New Year but unsure whether it would make the slightest difference. After all, she'd had an affair with the boss, nothing really new there. It was an age-old trend, hopefully a dying one she thought to herself as she took the first step upstairs and heard a huge tearing sound followed by giggles from Alison and outright laughter from Alistair.

'It's just not your day today, is it?' Alistair patted her on the shoulder.

'Just go home, Alisha.' Alison continued up the stairs as Alisha twisted round to find a huge split in her trousers and her knickers on view to the world. 'I'll tell Grandpa you're not feeling well.'

'But the meeting…' She hesitated, desperate to go home and curl up in bed till this awful day had ended yet hating to admit defeat.

'It will only be to go over the meeting we had earlier with the Walkers,' Alistair said, waiting on the top step for Alison. 'You know Grandpa likes to have meetings about meetings.'

'Make sure you tell him I'm throwing up or something like that.' Decision made; Alisha hurried back into her office to grab Alistair's coat which she had to wrap around her waist to cover the tear in her trousers. She kept her head down all the way so no one would see her and snuck out the back way so she could avoid the factory floor. Had she not done this she would have met Tom who had been dragging out leaving in the hope of catching Alisha but with the mess she was in perhaps that was a good thing.

Chapter 8

'It's all sorted, just the formal announcement to come and then we'll be in the food business too.' It was Valentine's Day and John had popped into the Jones' office as it was affectionately known to inform them of how things had been progressing.

'When's that happening then?' Alison asked, popping her head up from the computer.

'Easter,' John stated. 'Your grandpa and Mr Walker are organising a little celebration for the Thursday before Good Friday.'

'By Grandpa,' Alisha asked. 'Do you mean Marsha?' John nodded. 'Jesus Christ, that woman has got her fingers in so many pies she could market herself in Sainsburys,' Alison giggled.

'Can you believe how cold it is?' Alistair came into the office, rubbing his hands together and blowing on them. 'Anyone would think global warming didn't exist.'

'And you are late because?' John looked at his watch which Alisha knew would read ten thirty.

'Sorry, Uncle John.' He hung his coat on the coat stand that stood in the corner and flung himself into his chair. 'Daniel has been a nightmare the past few nights, we've put him in his own room and he's just not settling so I thought, as a valentine present, I'd let Sally have a lie in and make her breakfast in bed.'

'That's a lovely gesture, Alistair but you could have told one of us beforehand.' John gave him a stern look.

Alisha and Alison knew this was only half of the reason, the full reason for Alistair being late was due to the fact that at six o clock this morning he'd texted their 'sibling' WhatsApp group to say he'd completely forgotten it was Valentine's Day and what the fuck could he do? It had been Alison's suggestion to make breakfast in bed and Alisha suggested letting Sally have a lie in but neither of them had assumed it would mean he'd be late for work, although, they probably could have guessed.

'Renee was looking for you earlier, some problem with one of the machines and Martin wants a chat about the new paper supplier we've got, apparently the quality isn't as good as the last one we had.'

'That's because its half the bleeding price of that last lot and we get it delivered the next day rather than having to wait a week.' Alistair got out of his chair. 'I'll go and see them now.'

'We can't cut back on quality,' Alisha heard John say as he accompanied Alistair out of the office.

'That's twice now Martin has complained about the paper and I'm sure Renee has been on about the roller for weeks,' Alisha commented to Alison.

'Alistair needs to watch himself or Grandpa will be taking the ordering back off him.' Alison wheeled herself out from behind her desk so she could look at Alisha who sat opposite, Alistair's desk sat in between the two of them, facing the window. 'I'm still a little shocked he gave it to him in the first place.'

'We all were.' Alisha pushed her chair along the floor, it wasn't as gracefully done as Alison's as Alisha's chair from Marsha never arrived and so Uncle John had found her one in the storeroom that had seen much better days, Alisha was still promising herself that trip to Argos.

'Grandma has told him he needs to start slowing down and handing over some of the reins to us,' Alison remarked.

'Ha!' Alisha scoffed. 'I'll believe that when I bloody well see it.' If working nine to five instead of nine to five thirty was her grandpa's idea of slowing down, then she'd hate to see his idea of speeding up.

'You didn't hear it from me,' Alison's voice was almost a whisper. 'But I heard Uncle John and Auntie Marcie over Christmas chatting with Mum and Dad and Uncle John said that Grandma had insisted that Grandpa retire fully by the end of the year.

'Never!' Alisha was genuinely shocked. 'Do you think that's why he's being a bit, shall we say, extra bossy at the moment? Trying to make sure everything is in order before he leaves?'

'Could be,' Alison nodded. 'Perhaps Marsha can be our secretary then.' The pair of them burst out laughing. 'Speak of the devil.'

Marsha walked into the office carrying the largest bouquet of roses that Alisha had ever seen.

'Look what just arrived,' she said, making a point of sniffing each bloom. 'It's our one-year anniversary today as well, isn't he just the sweetest?'

'Sickeningly so,' Alison muttered under her breath, but Alisha heard and bit on her hand to stop herself from laughing.

'What was that?' Marsha shot her a scathing look. 'You're just jealous. I don't see any flowers on YOUR desk.'

'That's because I have no need of flowers to know how Richard feels about me,' Marsha laughed.

'Did he forget?' She pulled a rose out of her bouquet and handed it to Alison. 'Here, have one of these.' Alison just stared at her. 'I'll just leave it on your desk then. Would you like one, Alisha? I see your desk is empty too.'

'Not that it is any of your business.' Alisha could tell that Marsha had riled Alison, about time too she thought to herself. 'But Richard and I will be jetting off to Paris for the weekend. Can I bring you back a souvenir? Some sour grapes maybe?'

'Jason and I popped over there a couple of weeks ago on the Eurostar, he just surprised me, such a romantic.' She hugged the roses to her chest. 'Make sure you visit Café de Flore. Their French onion soup is just to die for.' And with that she sauntered out of the office.

'Is that all she came in for?' Alison stared at the closed door. 'To brag?'

'Of course,' Alisha shrugged her shoulders. 'I've been trying to tell you what she's like for ages, but you all think I'm jealous of her and Jason. Are you really going to Paris for the weekend? You never mentioned it.'

'Bloody well looks like I am now.' She shoved her chair back to her desk and started tapping away. 'How fucking much?'

'It's Valentine's weekend sis,' Alisha reminded her. 'What did you expect?'

'Oh, that's a shame.' She pulled her passport out of her bag. 'It's run out.'

'That's convenient,' Alisha laughed. 'Why have you got your passport anyway?' Alisha didn't even carry her driving license with her.

'Richard and I are volunteering at a children's hospice, and we need to have a DBS check first to check we're not horrible people, we're going after work.' Alisha's mouth fell open.

'That's how you're spending Valentine's night?' she shook her head.

'Richard's brother works there; we went last week and Alisha it's just heart wrenching, but they all just keep on smiling and if reading them a story or playing dolls with them means they forget the pain or their parents can go and have a quick cup of tea or a breath of fresh air then its bloody worth it.'

'Why the hell didn't you tell Marsha that? Instead of making up some bullshit about Paris.' Alisha smiled wryly at her. 'That would really have shut her up, she hasn't got a charitable bone in her body.'

'She just got my back up.' Alison looked over towards the window. 'Is that shouting?' The pair of them stood up and walked over to the window that overlooked the shop floor.

'You're not listening to a word I'm saying, Mr Jones.' It was Renee and Alistair. 'This roller is dangerous; the safety screen is cracked and for some reason the shut off button is not working fast enough. Look.' They watched as Renee hit the red emergency button, but the roller kept rolling for a few seconds when it should have instantly stopped. 'It needs to be condemned until it is fixed. Someone could lose a limb.'

'I understand perfectly, Miss Roberts, but unfortunately we cannot afford to be a machine down at the moment.' Alisha could see he was trying to make himself seem taller than he was. Alistair hadn't inherited the Frost height and Renee towered over him. 'We are already behind on our quotas for this week, we've had a lot of people off sick and we need to get on top of things.'

'That's it.' Renee slammed her clipboard down and Alisha watched as she stormed out of sight then heard angry footsteps marching up the stairs and into the office above. Alisha and Alison looked at the ceiling, they could hear raised voices but not quite what was being said but the fact that within half an hour, the roller machine in question was taped off and the engineer called meant that Renee had got her way.

'That bloody friend of yours,' Alistair came into their office, slamming the door behind him. 'Who does she think she is?'

'A supervisor,' Alisha answered. 'Who is in charge of making sure the machines are safe.'

'She's just doing her job Alistair,' Alison confirmed. 'That machine was playing up before Christmas. Why didn't you get it fixed earlier?'

'I forgot,' he said simply.

'You can't forget with things like this,' Alison scolded. 'It's people's lives.'

'She's exaggerating.' He waved his hand as if he were waving the situation away.

'I very much doubt it.' Alisha knew Renee was a hardworking and extremely conscientious worker. That's why she'd been promoted to supervisor at such a young age.

'Well you would stick up for her, wouldn't you?' he glared at her. 'I've had Grandpa and Uncle John on at me and now Uncle John is supervising me. What am I eight?'

Alisha was secretly quite glad that both her siblings were having enlightenments today, long may it last she thought.

'Is Marsha around?' Jason had appeared at the door, he looked mithered and appeared to be holding something behind his back.

'She was here a moment ago,' Alison replied while Alisha tried not to look at his handsome face, then saw the look of embarrassment on her brother's and smiled a little at how uncomfortable he would be feeling at this moment. It was very rare for Jason to come into their office. He usually dealt with Uncle John and now Marsha of course.

'She came to show us the lovely roses you sent her.' Alisha found some inner strength to actually answer him instead of cowering in the corner.

'Roses?' He seemed genuinely confused. 'I haven't sent her any roses.'

'You mean you didn't send a huge bunch of red roses here earlier?' Alisha was now wondering if Marsha had sent them to herself. 'The mystery begins.'

'I wanted to surprise her.' He pulled out a small bunch of pink carnations from behind his back that looked like the ones you got from a petrol station.

'Shall I help you find her?' Oh, this would be good Alisha thought to herself. 'Alison? Care to join me?'

'I would love to help you look for Marsha.' It was as if Alison had read Alisha's mind. 'She's probably upstairs, in fact…' She paused. 'I'm sure that's heels I can hear. Let's go and see, shall we?' Alison and Alisha led the way upstairs to their grandpa's office and sure enough, Marsha was there, pouring over some figures with Frost Senior and Junior.

'Jason?' Marsha rushed over to him and hugged him. 'What a lovely surprise and more flowers.' She took the carnations with a smile, but Alisha noticed it never reached her eyes.

'More flowers?' There was that confused look. 'Alisha said something about roses, but I thought she was winding me up.'

'Were those roses even for you?' Alison asked. 'Was there a card?'

'Of course, there wasn't a card, it's Valentine's Day.' Alisha wasn't sure she believed her.

'Shall we take another look?' Alisha was first out of the door and ran into Marsha's office next door. The smell of perfume was overwhelming, and she almost choked. 'Nothing on the flowers,' she said as all of the others except for her grandpa had joined her. 'Ah ha.' She spied what was quite obviously a florist's envelope under Marsha's table. Picking it up she read the name in disbelief. 'Alisha Frost.' She stared and stared at the name. 'But who would be sending flowers to me?'

Chapter 9

'Care to explain?' Alisha shoved the envelope under Marsha's nose.

'Well, I never actually said the roses were mine.' Alisha couldn't believe the nerve of Marsha.

'You bloody well did,' Alison piped in.

'No I didn't,' Marsha defended. 'I said, look what's just arrived, you both assumed they were for me.'

'Because you were holding them like they were the best thing since sliced bread.' Alisha tucked the card into her pocket and picked the bouquet up off Marsha's desk.

'Anyway, there isn't actually an Alisha Frost working here,' Alisha rolled her eyes.

'You're really using that as an excuse?' Alisha couldn't believe it. 'How many times do the three of us get post addressed to us as Frost and not Jones? Everyone just assumes we're Frost.' Alisha knew this meant the flowers were from someone who didn't know her very well, could they possible be from Tom? Dare she hope?

'Can someone please tell me why on earth you are all congregating in here when there's work to be done?' Grandpa Frost was standing in the doorway. 'Every single one of my management staff idling the morning away.' A whistle sounded from the factory floor. 'Well, you can all go without lunch break now.' And with those words he headed back into his office.

'Come on you lot.' Uncle John ushered them all out, leaving Marsha and Jason. 'Five minutes, Mr Wright, and you can be on your way too please.'

'She's got away with it again,' Alisha cried as the three of them walked back into their office. 'She needs to change her surname to Underhand.'

'Alisha, they're just flowers,' Alison sat down at her desk.

'Well, you've changed your tune,' Alisha remarked. 'A minute ago you were against her.'

'I was never against her.' Alison drank from a mug on her desk and grimaced at the cold tea. 'She's just a bit of an attention seeker that's all.'

'Like she said,' Alistair interrupted. 'You just assumed the roses were hers.' Alisha shook her head in disbelief and slumped down into her chair.

'Speaking of roses.' Alison inclined her head to the bouquet that now covered Alisha's entire desk. 'Who are they from?'

'No idea.' That wasn't strictly true, and she knew it.

'Don't be so obtuse, Alisha,' Alison scolded. 'What does the card say?'

'There isn't one.' Another lie, Alisha had felt a card inside when she'd placed it in her pocket. 'It's just my name.' No one else had seen the little envelope and Alisha intended to keep it that way until she could look at the card inside on her own.

'Bloody secret valentines,' Alistair muttered. 'Can't believe Grandpa banned our break. Is that even legal?'

'Considering you've only been in an hour and a half; you don't bloody need one anyway.' Alisha reached into her bag. 'Shortbread anyone?' The three of them munched on biscuits and a packet of wine gums that Alistair found in his desk until Uncle John came in with sandwiches and pop for them about thirty minutes later.

It wasn't until Alisha was sitting in her car that evening ready to drive home that she remembered the card.

'To match your dress.' Was all it said, but this was more than enough for Alisha, and she knew exactly who had sent them. She looked behind her and smiled at them on the back seat and then as she looked back to the front, her smile grew.

Tom was leaning against the wall of the factory, under one of the spotlights, dressed in a black winter coat, the collar raised around his neck to ward off the cold chill of the coming night. 'I see you got my roses.'

'Thank you, they're beautiful.' She walked over to him in what she hoped was a sultry manner.

'Like you,' he said as she approached and tucked a wisp of hair behind her ear. 'You haven't got a coat on,' he stated, mistaking her shiver of anticipation for one of cold. 'Come here.' He unbuttoned his coat and held it open for her to step inside. It didn't quite cover the both of them and the chill on her back was so noticeable against the heat that now radiated from him at the front of her body, but she wouldn't have moved for all the tea in China.

'Much better.' She nestled into his neck, inhaling the faint smell of aftershave he must have applied that morning.

'I came to ask you out for dinner,' he whispered into her ear. 'Anywhere round here we can go?'

'There's a few places but I bet they'll all be fully booked.' She didn't want to move from this spot all evening. She'd quite happily stand in the factory car park all night if it meant she could be this close to him. 'It is Valentine's Day, you know,' he laughed, and she felt his Adam's apple move against her cheek.

'But people still need to eat.' He pushed her gently away from him and she felt the cold hit her like a wet fish in the face. 'Have you got a jacket in the car?' She nodded, walked quickly to her car, grabbed her fleecy coat and bag, and locked the car back up.

'We could try Leonardo's?' It was the first restaurant she could think of. 'Do you like Italian?'

'Who doesn't like pasta smothered in sauce and cheese?' He took her hand and even through the gloves he was wearing she could feel the warmth from his skin. 'Lead the way.'

Leonardo's was, as Alisha had suspected fully booked, so was Pizza Hut, The Stonegate and the fifties diner.

'McDonalds?' she joked as she saw the familiar golden arches.

'I could just go a Big Mac and banana milkshake right about now.' She looked up at him and realised he was serious.

'McDonalds it is then.' After all, she thought to herself, she had been heading home to a microwave meal for one and a night in front of the TV so a burger and fries in the company of Tom felt like afternoon tea at the Ritz.

Inside was busy for a weekday evening and an inordinate amount of couples seemed to be occupying the tables rather than the usual mix of teenagers and families.

'Looks like they couldn't get into the posh places either?' Tom nodded towards a couple who were dressed to the nines, seated at a table in the window, slurping milkshakes.

'They might be going to the theatre,' Alisha commented as they stood in the queue. 'I'm sure I saw a poster saying the ballet was in town this week.'

'How can I help you?' The lady smiled at them both as they reached the counter.

'Big Mac meal with a banana milkshake, 6 chicken nuggets, a cheeseburger and two apple pies please.' Alisha wasn't sure whether Tom ordering for her was sweet and romantic or just annoying. 'Your turn?'

'That's all for you?' Alisha looked at him.

'I'm bloody starving,' he replied. 'In fact, make it a large meal please.' The lady nodded before turning to Alisha.

'Quarter pounder meal please with a cup of tea.' As much as she loved milkshakes, she'd suddenly realised her feet were freezing in her work shoes and she needed something hot to drink.

After paying and collecting their trays, they headed over to a table by the window that had just been vacated.

'Not quite what I had in mind for the evening,' Tom said, as they opened their burger boxes and tipped their fries into the lids.

'It's better than anything else I had planned,' she smiled at him, and he smiled back before taking a huge bite of burger and splattering sauce down her chin.

'Here,' he handed her a serviette which she took graciously.

'Is it gone?' she asked, wiping her chin, and hoping she hadn't spilt any on her coat, it was her favourite.

'Just a bit there,' he pointed.

'Gone?' Alisha rubbed at her chin again.

'Come here.' Tom took another serviette and gently dabbed at her chin, never taking his eyes from hers. Never had something as mundane as having sauce wiped off your chin felt so wonderfully intimate and romantic. 'All gone.' Tom's voice sounded huskier than normal as their eyes broke contact, and he picked up his burger again.

'Thank you,' she said, lowering her lashes in case he could see the desire in them.

'What do you fancy doing next then?' he took a slurp of milkshake, the noise making Alisha giggle slightly. 'Is there a cinema here? Bowling alley maybe?'

'There's a roller rink a few streets away.' Alisha loved roller skating, ever since she'd been to a birthday party for one of her school friends at the age of ten.

'I've never been in my life,' Tom admitted. 'I had a pair of those ones you wore over your shoes once but that's about it.'

'It's great fun.' The fact that Tom hadn't been before made it an even better idea in Alisha's opinion, it meant he'd need to hold onto her, a lot.

'Roller skating it is then,' he smiled at her, such a huge smile that she felt her insides melting and had to avert her eyes once more just in case he could read her mind.

'Right, we'll stick to the outside for now, by the barrier. If you have one hand on there and hold on to me the other side, you'll soon get the hang of it.' The roller rink was busier than Alisha had expected it to be. The 'expert' skaters were busy showing off their skills, cornering with ease and skating backwards at every opportunity.

'How do you even do that?' Tom watched one particular skater jump a ramp that was set up in the middle and execute a perfect twist before landing elegantly and skating off to line himself up for another go.

'Practise,' Alisha said simply as she took his hand. 'Just sort of push with each foot and...'

'Like this?' Tom interrupted and pushed off from the barrier before letting go of her hand and skating around her.

'You bloody liar.' She went to slap him but lost her footing, tripped on the stopper, and fell into his arms. 'Where did you learn to skate?'

'A mis spent youth at the skate park.' He caught her easily, holding onto her arms for much longer than was necessary before lifting her up onto her skates and placing a gentle kiss on the tip of her nose.

'Right then people.' The DJ in the centre of the rink had turned the lights down and put on a slow song. 'This is for all the love birds out there. Happy Valentine's Day.'

'May I have this dance?' Tom held out his hand which Alisha took with a smile and together they skated slowly round and round to I will always love you by Whitney Houston.

The night was over all too soon and before she knew it, they were back in the factory car park.

'I've had such a lovely evening.' They were standing by her car, but Alisha was reluctant to get in, even though she was freezing cold. The chill of the evening had turned into a thick frost and covered everything in white sparkles. She shivered and this time it was from the cold.

'In you get,' he said, opening her door and ushering her inside. 'Where's your scraper?' He looked on the back seat and smiled at the roses.

'It's here,' she handed him the ice scraper from the passenger side door that she'd finally remembered to buy after snapping her credit card in two.

'Get the engine running and I'll get some of this off for you.' Alisha did as she was told and watched Tom as he scraped the ice from the windscreen, leaving the back as it had already melted from the rear window heater. 'You're all set.' He handed the scraper back to her through the now open window.

'Thank you,' was all she could think to say. 'Where's your car?' What a stupid question, she thought to herself, she didn't really care where his car was, she just wanted to ask him when she'd be able to see him again.

'Just round the corner,' he smiled and reached in to touch her cheek gently. 'I've had a lovely evening too.' He leant in through the window and placed a firm but short kiss on her lips. 'I'll see you soon.' And with that he placed his hands in his pockets and all she could do was watch him walk out of the car park and turn right by the gates. By the time she had recovered herself and driven through them herself there was no sign of him.

Chapter 10

'It's all wonderfully romantic if you ask me,' Renee said the following weekend when the girls had all met for lunch and a catch up. 'Roses, surprise dates.'

'Bloody frustrating more like,' Lizzie quipped, breaking a corner from her sandwich. They were seated in their favourite coffee shop in the town centre, overlooking the canal that ran straight through the middle of the town. 'She's met him three times now, knows hardly anything about him and has no idea when or if she's ever going to see him again.'

'Of course she's going to see him again.' Renee was forever the optimist.

'How can you be so sure?' Fay asked. 'Not one of their meetings have been planned.'

'Because of the business,' Renee stated matter of factly. 'Surely they'll meet at some point.'

'But I don't want to meet him at some point.' Alisha was busy pretending to eat her cheese toastie but was really just pushing it around her plate. 'I want to go on dates with him, ring him up, send seductive texts. I can't even bloody email him.'

'It's a bit shit really, isn't it?' Lizzie said.

'Thank you, Captain Obvious,' Alisha looked at her. 'That's what I've been saying.'

'You'll definitely see him at Easter.' Renee patted her hand reassuringly. 'When the merger gets announced officially,' she told Fay and Lizzie who had looked at her with blank expressions.

'But that's weeks away,' Alisha cried out in despair. 'I don't think I can wait that long.'

In the end, it was actually only two weeks that Alisha had to wait. Coming back into the office after a trip to the bauble department one Tuesday morning, she heard her name mentioned.

'Alisha can do what exactly?' she asked her Uncle John.

'Go to Walkers and help with the accounts system.' Alison was grinning at her as if she'd planned the whole thing. 'Marsha was going but she's in bed with the flu apparently so it's up to you little sis.'

'But I can't…' She desperately wanted to but setting up a whole new system scared the life out of her. 'Hang on, I thought they didn't have technology and stuff like that.'

'Who on earth told you that?' Uncle John looked at her. 'They're a religious family with an extremely close-knit community but not have technology?' *Did this mean Tom had a mobile?* Alisha asked herself. 'Their current system is old fashioned and outdated and it needs to be on the same level as ours for ordering and stock levels.'

'I'll have to take Alistair.' Alisha looked at her brother for help. 'He's the best when it comes to computers and things.'

'Already done, Alisha.' Alistair had the same grin on his face as Alison. 'I was there all last week, setting everything up, installing the new computers. It just needs your touch now,' he winked at her.

'But you know about the accounts as well as I do.' She didn't really know why she was so reluctant to go, she was itching to see Tom again but on the other hand she didn't want the responsibility of new account systems especially as she still hadn't got the hang of it here at Frosts.

'You're going and that's that.' Uncle John walked out of the office. 'Mr Walker and his son are expecting you within the hour.' Alisha didn't see the knowing smile he gave to Alison and Alistair as he went out.

'Jesus, Alisha!' Alistair whistled through his teeth. 'Anyone would think you didn't want to go and see him.'

'It's not that.' Alisha was getting butterflies at the thought of Tom's handsome face; would he greet her with a kiss perhaps? 'I'm having enough trouble with the bloody system here, how can I set up a new one over there?'

'You don't have to.' Alison grinned again. 'Alistair and Marsha did it all last week. We just concocted a plan with Uncle John when we heard Marsha was off today.'

'She should have been going over to do the finishing touches but now you can.' Alistair finished off the story, leaned back in his chair and placed his feet on the table in a pleased with himself manner. 'It's nothing you can't do, just set up a few user IDs and passwords, transfer the old account details to the new system and voila.'

'Get Tom's number,' Alison butted in, and Alisha blushed. 'I see that idea has had the desired effect.'

'Well then, Miss Jones.' Alistair stood up and grabbed her coat from the coat stand and held it out to her. 'Time to get your man.'

'We weren't expecting you, Miss Frost,' Mr Walker greeted Alisha at the door to the factory, it was a lot smaller than Frosts with a delicious aroma of baking that seemed to seep out of its walls.

'It's Jones,' she corrected, taking his outstretched hand, and shaking it warmly. 'But honestly, just call me Alisha.' He opened the door for her and led her through the reception, smiling and waving at the woman behind the desk who waved back whilst talking on the phone and into another office where two gleaming new computers sat on old fashioned desks. 'Marsha has been taken ill I'm afraid, so I've come to get you up and running.'

'Then we are honoured indeed.' She turned to find Tom leaning against another doorway at the opposite end of the office.

'Tom my boy,' Mr Walker waved him inside. 'You remember Alisha, don't you?'

'How could I forget?' He smiled as he walked over to her, and it took all of her strength to keep standing upright because her knees felt like they would collapse at any minute.

'Why don't you give Miss…I mean Alisha here a little tour and I'll get us a nice cup of tea ready for when you get back.' Mr Walker rubbed his hands together. 'I think Johnny brought us a fresh batch of shortbread in this morning.'

Alisha put her bag down, next to one of the computers and followed Tom out of the door she had first come through, back into the reception and then through double doors into a changing room.

'You need to be properly attired for this.' He handed her a white coat, hat, and hair net which she donned quickly while he did the same, before opening another door which led onto the factory floor.

The smell that hit Alisha's nose was intense and delicious. It reminded her of the many afternoons she'd spent as a child, baking biscuits and cakes with Alison and Alistair and their grandma. Unlike Frosts, this factory was completely open plan and Alisha could immediately see where each part of the process took place. Huge chrome mixing bowls stood on one side with metal ladders leading up to platforms. Tom informed her that was where the ingredients were poured in.

Some of the mixing bowls poured their contents into massive pipes and others had their mixtures tipped out depending on what was inside, Tom explained. There were machines that cut biscuits and other machines that dolloped cake batter into waiting tins. Then there were huge ovens, the heat from these was intense as they passed through.

'Where does the decorating happen?' They had already come to the labelling and boxing part of the factory, but Alisha hadn't seen any sign of icing.

'We don't do that yet,' Tom explained as they went back into the changing room and took off the protective clothing. 'There's a part of the factory at the back that we always intended to use but never got round to it. All the equipment is coming next week and then soon we'll be decorating Christmas cakes and gingerbread galore.'

'Are you ok with all the changes?' She'd noticed a hint of sadness in his voice. 'Not everyone likes Christmas.'

'We're employing ten more people from May, and we've never had so many orders,' he shrugged his shoulders. 'It's not ideal, but if it means Walkers can continue trading then it's fine by me.' He reached out to take her hand. 'Plus, it means I get to spend time with you.' He pulled her in towards him, her body touching every inch of his. 'I'm definitely ok with those changes.' He tilted his head, searching her eyes for permission. Closer his lips came, closer and closer until they were upon hers with the lightest of touches.

'Oh Tom,' she moaned, and this was all the permission he needed as his mouth claimed hers in a kiss filled with hunger and longing.

'I've been wanting to do that since the ball,' he pulled away, his breath ragged and uneven.

'And I've been wanting you to.' She squeezed his hand, delight coursing through her as she realised he felt exactly the same as she did. *Could she actually be this lucky?*

They headed towards the door but as Alisha went to take Tom's hand, he snatched his away.

'I'm sorry,' he explained. 'It's just Mum and Dad are big sticklers for propriety and all that stuff.'

'I understand.' She didn't really and she felt down and disheartened all of a sudden.

'Soon,' he promised and placed a kiss on the top of her head before they walked out of the door and back into the office.

The day passed quickly and without any chance of further kisses due to Mr Walker being an extremely hands-on boss and wanting to know everything about everything.

'What kind of a boss would I be if I didn't know how it all worked,' he had said, before asking Alisha to explain the basics about each system. She found it all relatively simple and wondered why she was having so much trouble with the one back at Frosts and she was hoping that by going back to basics here, it would help her sort out the problems with her own accounts.

Before she knew it, it was five o' clock and time for her to leave. Mr Walker insisted on accompanying her to her car and loitered until she was in the car with the engine running, literally about to take off.

'Any problems just give us a ring,' Alisha called out of the window. 'Here's my number.' She suddenly remembered what Alison had said about getting Tom's number and she fumbled in her bag for a business card and handed it to Tom.

'Thank you again for coming out and helping.' Mr Walker took the card from Tom's hand and tucked it away into his jacket packet. 'Tell your grandfather we are very much looking forward to working with you all.' And still he loitered. A helpless look crossed Tom's face and in the end, she gave up, said a final goodbye before putting the window up and driving out.

As she reached the gates, she glanced into her rear-view mirror, Mr Walker had turned to head back into the factory, but Tom remained, staring after the car. She turned around in her seat to look out of the back window and caught the kiss he blew her with her hand and took it to her heart.

Chapter 11

'Are you telling me that you still don't have the man's number?' Alisha and Renee were whiling away an hour or two in the coffee shop next to the factory after a power cut that morning had caused the factory to close and all the staff except for management had been sent home for an early start to the weekend.

'No,' Alisha shook her head in despair. 'I completely forgot when I first got there, thought I had a few hours but then his dad was there all the time and I mean all the time.' She emphasised all, both times.

'Perhaps he suspects,' Renee stirred the cream into her hot chocolate.

'Don't be silly.' Alisha had opted for a double espresso; she was confident she'd need the caffeine hit later on.

'What's silly about it?' Renee waved the wooden stirrer at her, flicking liquid onto Alisha's sleeve.

'Renee!'

'Sorry,' she dabbed at Alisha's sleeve. 'I'm serious though, I saw you two at the ball and you couldn't take your eyes off each other and that was the first time you met. I dread to think what the sexual tension is like now.'

'You are being silly,' Alisha scoffed. 'Sexual tension indeed.' She took a bite out of the crumbly biscuit. 'There's more sexual tension in my little finger.' She wagged her finger at Renee to drum her point home. 'I told you what happened when I went to take his hand.'

'You did,' Renee agreed. 'But you also told me about the hot kiss in the changing room and the sweet thing he did when you drove off. So don't try dampening it down now my girl.'

'It's not going to go anywhere though, is it?' Alisha had mulled over the past few weeks. 'If his parents are that religious, stuck up, whatever it is, they're not going to be very happy with their precious son being with me, are they? I'm about as religious as the devil.'

'Has he said he doesn't want to be with you?' Alisha shook her head. 'In fact he's said the very opposite and you're just being a big grump about it.'

'Hark at you,' Alisha retorted. 'What were you like waiting for David to ask you out? You were a sour puss for weeks.'

'We're not talking about me.' Renee put her hand up, palm towards Alisha, signalling an end to the current conversation. 'We are talking about you and Tom and your lack of ambition in finding a way of contacting him. Surely someone has his mobile.'

'We only have the office phone and email,' Alisha shrugged.

'Just phone the office and ask to speak to him.' Renee pulled her mobile phone out. 'Honestly, Alisha, I don't think you have a brain sometimes.' She clicked on a few things then all of a sudden Alisha could hear a phone ringing. 'Yes, hello, it's Renee here from Frosts. I was wondering if I could speak with Tom, please.' A pause. 'Oh, that's unfortunate. Could I have his mobile number please? It's imperative I speak with him as soon as possible.' Another pause. 'No, I don't think Mr Walker can help, it really does need to be Tom.' Renee started scribbling down numbers on a pen that had appeared as if by magic. 'Thank you very much. Goodbye.' She pushed what Alisha discovered to be an old cinema ticket with hastily scribbled numbers on. 'And that my dear, is how you get someone's number.' She sat back in her chair with a smug smile on her face.

'Power's back on.' Alisha nodded towards the lights that were now shining through the factory windows that could be seen from the coffee shop.

'Thank you, Renee,' Renee said sarcastically.

'Thank you, Renee,' Alisha mimicked as the pair of them hastily finished their drinks and headed out of the warm shop and back into the March air.

'It's five o' clock,' Renee moaned as they walked back into the factory through the back shutters and past the clocking in and out machine. 'I should be at home now, soaking in the bath with a large gin.' The factory was silent as they walked past the machines and back into the offices. 'What's the point of an early Friday finish if you have to stay late?'

'There you both are,' Uncle John was waiting for them. 'Renee, will you and Martin make sure all the machines are turned off properly, we'll sort any issues out on Monday when we have full staff back in. Then lock up and get yourselves home.' Renee nodded to him and Alisha and went off to find Martin.

'I'll go and get my stuff and get home.' Alisha went to walk past him, but he took her arm gently.

'Bit of a problem with the computers, I'm afraid.' She walked beside him as they came to her office. Alison and Alistair were both in front of their screens, looks of absolute horror on their faces.

'They've completely and utterly crashed.'

'Mine won't even switch on.'

Alisha rushed to her desk and discovered the same fate had befallen hers.

'I had two orders that needed to be in,' Alison complained.

'I was in the middle of the timesheets,' Alisha sat in her chair with a flump. 'What do we do?'

'There won't be any repair places open now,' Uncle John stated. 'We'll have to wait until Monday and hope it can be fixed.'

'Grandpa will go mad,' Alistair commented. 'It will be bad enough when he finds out about the power cut but now the computers have gone down.'

'He'll never go on holiday again,' Alison said. 'It took Grandma and Aunt Marcie months to persuade him to go on that cruise and as soon as he's out of the country, this happens.'

'We don't need to tell him.' Three faces looked at Alisha in shock. 'What? He can't do anything about it, and it will only ruin their holiday.' The three faces relaxed a little as they considered what she was saying. 'I'm not saying don't tell him ever but why tell him now? Let's all chill a little, go home and call the computer people first thing Monday morning. In fact, I'll ring them now just in case and leave a message if no one is there.'

'When did you get so smart?' Alistair teased, grabbing his coat, and picking up his briefcase.

'I always have been, you've just never noticed,' Alisha laughed, waving goodbye to everyone as she googled local computer experts on her phone and promised to lock up.

'Still here, Alisha?' Marsha sauntered past the office. The two of them had never been friends but since the Valentine's Day incident, conversations between the two of them had been frosty to say the least.

'Just trying to find someone to come out on Monday to fix whatever it is that needs fixing.' She didn't even look up from her phone.

'I think it's a good idea not to tell Mr Frost.' Alisha hadn't realised that Marsha was standing right in front of her and jumped a little at the closeness of her voice. 'John told me not to say anything,' Alisha nodded. 'He's not quite as strong as everyone wants him to think you know.' And with that statement she wished Alisha a good night and walked out, leaving Alisha in utter bewilderment as to what had actually just happened.

Monday morning arrived to find the three Joneses, Uncle John and Marsha all arriving early along with the morning shift at six. The factory worked an early and a late shift, Monday to Thursday with an early finish on the Friday as long as all the work was done, and Alisha couldn't remember a week when the work hadn't been done. As her grandpa always told her, look after your workers and they will look after you.

And it was true. There was very little sickness that wasn't a genuine illness or issues with childcare. The factory floor was, for the most part, a happy place to be and everyone agreed that Frosts were firm but fair employees. Overtime was rare except in the run up to Christmas, but it was paid at double time and rewarded with a factory wide shut down.

Alisha watched the employees arriving, all of them happy and chatting to each other, ready for a day's work. Unlike Alisha who dreaded Monday mornings. She hadn't always felt this way. In fact, up until recently she'd loved coming to work regardless of the day and would often stay late or arrive early. But since the arrival of Marsha and the new systems it seemed to have all changed.

She'd always had to work harder than her siblings to prove herself. She was the youngest and therefore the less experienced but her grandpa's attitude towards her lately and everyone's willingness to bend over backwards to accommodate Marsha was really starting to grate on her and cause her some genuine concerns. And the issues she was having with the new systems just added to her problems.

Soon the hum of the machines could be heard, and they left them in the capable hands of the workers and headed off to await the arrival of the computer repair man who Alisha had managed to make contact with on Friday just as he was leaving his own office. Sean had promised to be at the factory for eight o' clock and bang on the dot he was there. After copious amounts of tea, most of the morning and countless ums and oh dears, there came a hallelujah moment when Sean declared the system had been infected by a particularly nasty virus but that luckily it was fixable, and he'd be able to reset all the computers and apply the backups to bring them back to where they were.

Alisha's face fell at the words 'back up'. She'd been having so much trouble lately that she'd forgotten to do a physical back up for a week at least and now she'd have to repeat all that work and receive more tuts and looks from her family.

It was just after lunch that Sean declared the computers ready to be used again.

'I noticed your back up wasn't quite up to date.' He took Alisha to one side. 'I've done my best to try and get some of the information back off the hard drive, but it's still only dated 28th February I'm afraid. Looks like the last viable back up was when you did your month end.'

'But that's almost all of March?' Alisha shrieked quietly. 'It's the wages at the end of the week, how am I ever going to get all that done?'

'I would suggest owning up and asking for help.' Was it that obvious to him that she was trying to hide something?

'Either that or you're going to have to put some serious overtime in.'

'Thank you for fixing them,' she said and shook his hand. 'We'll get the bill paid as soon as possible. After all, you came out so quickly to help.'

In the end, Alisha decided a little fabrication of the truth was the best policy and she told her siblings that her backups weren't viable and could they help input the past few weeks work. It wasn't strictly a lie and even with their help, the wages were only just in on time. But, lesson learnt, Alisha backed up her computer every time she switched it off from then on.

Chapter 12

'Are you coming, Alisha?' Uncle John popped his head round the office door. 'Alison and Alistair are already there and Dad's waiting in the car for me and you.'

'I can't get the figures to balance, Uncle John.' It was the end of March and Alisha had been working on the payroll for the financial year end. It was the first year processing the new software that Marsha had insisted they all started using and month by month the figures hadn't matched and now she was almost ten thousand pounds out. Alisha was positive it couldn't be right, had she inputted something on the debit side instead of the credit or vice versa?

'Leave it for now, little one,' Uncle John soothed. 'It's not going anywhere. It will still be here after the bank holiday.'

'But Uncle John?' Alisha whined.

'No buts, Alisha.' He moved into the office and placed his finger over the off button of the computer. 'Is it saved?' she nodded, and the computer closed down. 'You need to be there with us all. This is a big deal for everyone in the company. We've closed early for this, and you know your grandpa never closes early.'

'Can't I just come along later?' She looked up hopefully.

'What's the matter?' He sat down opposite her. 'You've been ever so strange for a while now. You didn't come to anything that was organised last year, but I was hoping after the Christmas party you'd start coming out of your shell again. I know it must be hard working with Marsha now she's seeing Jason, but you've got to move on.'

'I know, Uncle John.' If only he knew the truth, she thought to herself. And this time it really wasn't that she didn't want to go, if she was being brutally honest, she couldn't wait to go. Tom would be there for starters. But she just hated leaving something unfinished.

'Come on then,' he said and tapped the desk. 'Switch off for the weekend…four whole days off work.'

'And Easter at Mum's!' she stuck her tongue out.

'Now, now,' he said and placed an arm round her shoulders as they walked out of the door and down the stairs. 'Your mum tries her best.'

'I think she does it on purpose, Uncle John.' Alisha turned off the lights as they made their way down the stairs. 'How can anyone ruin a roast dinner year after year?'

'Well if she's doing it to avoid cooking each year then she isn't doing a very good job is she?' Uncle John jangled his keys as he found the one for the main door. 'How many years have we been going to your parents' house for Easter now?'

'Since before I was born.' Alisha waved at her grandpa who was now honking the horn of his Jaguar at them both and tapping his watch.

'Coming, Dad,' Uncle John shouted. He turned the key in the lock, tried the handle twice then with the help of Alisha they both pulled down the shutter and Uncle John clicked on the padlock. The rest of the factory was already shuttered and locked, all the employees having left over an hour ago.

'What took you so long?' Grandpa Frost had already started the engine and was beginning to drive off before Alisha and Uncle John had even got their seat belts on.

'Sorry, Grandpa,' Alisha apologised. 'It was my fault. I was struggling to balance the end of year wages and I hate leaving things unfinished.'

'Well from what Marsha has been telling me you've been struggling a lot lately.' He negotiated the tight bend that led to the main road with ease as he spoke. 'I think we need to sit down and have a proper chat young lady.'

'Yes, Grandpa.' Alisha sank deeper into the leather seats feeling like a child and wished the car would swallow her up so she could disappear.

'Don't be too hard on her, Dad,' Uncle John always tried to smooth things over. 'It's been a tough year for her.'

'Tough?' Grandpa Frost tutted. 'Kids these days don't know the meaning of the word tough.' He tapped his fingers impatiently on the steering wheel as they waited for traffic lights to change. 'I worked fourteen-hour days to get this factory to where it is today. We didn't have computers and technology to help. Software for this, software for that. I had a ledger and a pen and not once didn't my books balance.' He sped off from the lights as soon as they turned green.

'It's the new system, Grandpa.' Alisa felt like she needed to say something. 'I never had any problems with Sage.'

'A bad workman always blames his tools.' Grandpa Frost turned the radio on signalling an end to the conversation, so Alisha pulled out her phone. 'And you can put that blasted thing away as well.' Even Uncle John appeared shocked at this comment. 'Honestly, all you lot do is go on your phones. Try actually talking to people or looking at the world through your own eyes rather than through a screen all the time.'

'Yes, Grandpa.' Alisha didn't have a clue what had gotten into him lately. He'd always been a bit of a tyrant but a sweet natured one all the same.

'Damn and blast,' he exclaimed and pulled over with a sudden halt. 'I've taken a wrong turn. I'm sure it was left at Richmond Road. Can you remember John?'

'Shall I check the SAT NAV on my phone, Grandpa?' This earned her a rather scornful look, but she smiled smugly to herself all the same and settled back into the seat, plugged her headphones in and hummed along to George Ezra's latest.

It was about another half an hour before they reached Walker & Son. It was a much smaller but more modern factory than Frosts. If Alisha remembered correctly, it had been built at the turn of the millennium compared to the mid twentieth century building that her grandpa had purchased back in the sixties.

Huge frames of glass were wide open to let in the early spring sunshine in complete contrast to the tiny panes that passed for windows at Frosts. The factory floor was always too hot or too cold and only the recent introduction of air conditioning in the offices had made them a more bearable place to work.

Grandpa Frost pulled into the first available parking space, totally ignoring the notice that read 'Director'. Mr Walker, a lady Alisha assumed to be Mrs Walker and Marsha were all standing outside a big red door and a huge sign that shouted 'Reception'. The two 'Walkers' came over to the car and much shaking of hands and introductions were made as Marsha smiled from the door. Alisha tried desperately not to ask after Tom and assumed that he was inside.

'Tom isn't here I'm afraid,' Marsha said slyly as they approached the door.

'And that bothers me because?' Alisha cursed inwardly.

'Don't give me that 'I'm not bothered' attitude,' she whispered snidely. 'It's written all over your face.'

'You have such a vivid imagination, Marsha.' Alisha hoped to God that it wasn't written all over her face. This was the main reason she'd allowed Uncle John to drag her away from her desk. The thought of seeing Tom again was a big enough incentive for her to leave the unbalanced payroll for another day.

'Pull the other one,' she laughed. 'It's got mistletoe on it.'

'You do realise it's a bell.' Alisha wasn't sure if Marsha was being deliberately thick or not.

'What's a bell?'

'Pull the other one…' she hinted. 'It's got a bell on it?'

'Of course, I know that,' Marsha shrugged her shoulders. 'Just trying to be original.'

'There's being original and then there's just being a thick bitc…Yes, Mrs Walker, such lovely weather we're having for the time of year.' Alisha stepped in beside Mrs Walker who had paused briefly to allow her to catch up.

'Please call me Mary.' Her tightly permed hair bobbed as she nodded her head towards Alisha. 'And I'm so sorry my boy isn't here. A little trouble in paradise I'm afraid.'

'Nothing too serious I hope?' Alisha didn't like the sound of this.

'We do hope not,' Mary placed a hand on her arm. 'Katie is such a good girl from a suitable family.'

'Katie?' Alisha's hopes were falling faster than a tart's knickers.

'Katie Sutherland,' Mary explained. 'Her father is the pastor of our church. Tom's been engaged to her since they were eighteen.'

'Engaged!' If Alisha had been drinking at that moment, she would have spat it out all over Mary's pristine pale blue dress.

'Dear Katie, is such a sweet girl.' Alisha could hear the malice in Marsha's tone. 'I do hope the wedding isn't going to be postponed?'

'Wedding!' This was too much for Alisha. 'Excuse me, Mary. I've come over all flushed.' She apologised and started walking back towards the door, her dreams shattered and her heart in pieces.

Chapter 13

Easter Monday found Alisha parking up outside the factory.
After the celebrations of Thursday's merger and three whole
days in the company of her mother and her ever sniping
grandfather, she'd had enough. Making her excuses the
previous evening she had gone back home and despite
herself had done nothing but think about Tom and his fiancé.
When finally dawn had arrived, she jumped in the car and
drove to the factory in dire need of a diversion and with a
steely determination to balance the year end payroll and get
the new tax year up and running.

She'd forgotten to get the main office key from Uncle John
so instead she had to unlock the huge shutter at the back of
the factory. Luckily it was now electric, so she pressed the
button until it had rolled up enough for her to duck under
then pressed the button to roll it back down and it slammed
and clattered into place.

With the shutter down it was almost pitch black in the
factory. What little sunlight there was outside had no chance
of penetrating through onto the shop floor and Alisha
wished, not for the first time and probably not for the last
that her grandpa had allowed Uncle John to make
improvements to the windows a few years back, but it was
seen as an unnecessary expense and like with many other
things, was put to the back of everyone's mind and never
mentioned again.

Grandpa Frost had never been one for change, especially anything that cost money which is why they had all been shocked when he had allowed Marsha to spend thousands on new payroll and account systems. But all he ever said was it would save us time and money in the long run. Money maybe but certainly not time, well Alisha's time anyway. She'd never spent so long balancing figures in her life, and she'd lost count of the amount of pounds she'd found herself just writing off and dumping in the suspense account, hoping that at the year-end it would all finally work out.

Pulling out her phone and switching on the torch she started to walk towards the top end of the factory. It was eerily quiet. The huge machines that printed the wrapping paper stood along the far wall, huge rolls of red, green, and gold waiting to be moved into the warehouse for storage. She ducked under the metal loops where the workers hung strand after strand of tinsel. Alisha loved visiting the factory when it was closed, there was a kind of peaceful tranquillity in the usually busy and noisy atmosphere being so silent and still. And no matter whether the factory was full of workers or empty as it was today it always felt like coming home.

She resisted the urge to walk through the other departments, promising to treat herself to a quick peek at the baubles on her way out and instead headed straight up the stairs to her office, stopping in the kitchen for a drink on the way. She instantly pushed the memory of her, and Tom's almost kiss out of her mind and busied herself with making tea and grabbing a couple of biscuits.

Five hours, three cups of coffee, numerous thumping of hands and throwing of pens later and Alisha finally seemed to be getting somewhere. She'd managed to narrow it down to the statutory payments that had been paid throughout the year but there were still major discrepancies between the computerised figures and the figures that had been submitted to the Revenue.

'I never had this problem with Sage,' she said for what felt like the hundredth time that day.

'Do you always talk to yourself?' Alisha almost jumped out of her skin and turned to find Tom standing in the doorway.

'Bloody hell!' She placed a hand over her heart which was beating ten to the dozen and not just because of the fright he'd just given her.

'I'm so sorry.' His face was pure concern. 'I didn't mean to startle you. It's just when I saw the shutters unlocked, I thought someone would be in here. I completely forgot it was a bank holiday, I've been so preoccupied the past few days since...' He trailed off.

'It's just me here.' Alisha ignored the sad look in his brown eyes and tried to remember everything his mother and Marsha had said about Katie. 'If you're looking for Grandpa or Uncle John, then they won't be back in until tomorrow.'

'I was looking for you Alisha,' he said and walked further into the room.

'And you found me.' She couldn't help the coolness in her voice despite the overwhelming desire to run into his arms.

'I've called it off.'

'Called what off?'

'You know full well what,' he said, smiling shyly at her but still she played dumb. 'My engagement.'

'And that concerns me because…' Had he really? Her heart was thumping once again.

'Not a second has passed that I haven't thought about you since our kiss under the mistletoe.' He was right in front of her desk now and she had to strain her neck to look up at him. 'I tried to push you from my mind, you don't know how much I've tried but then when I saw you at that meeting all tangled up in your jumper and fighting with your bag I just knew.'

'Knew what exactly?' Oh lord did he have to remind her about that day.

'That I couldn't marry Katie,' he took hold of her hands. 'It was never a love match anyway, not on either side. It was what our parents wanted and as neither of us had any real objections we just allowed it to happen but since meeting you…' He looked coyly at his shoes. 'Since meeting you, I've felt very, very different.'

'In what way?' She stood up and stepped around the side of the desk while still keeping hold of his hands.

'Do I have to spell it out?' His eyes seemed darker all of a sudden, like hot chocolate on a winter's night. His lips were parted slightly, and she noticed him lick them nervously.

'It might be nice for you to spell it out.' She sidled in between him and the desk, so they were almost but not quite touching. 'I mean, I'm still a little confused you know.' She smiled what she hoped was her most flirtatious smile and was rewarded by him moving even closer towards her, so close that every part of their bodies were touching.

'From the moment I saw you, Alisha, I was transfixed,' he grasped her hands tighter in one of his. 'I stepped into the room that night and there you were. That tight red dress you wore and the way you smiled, took my breath away.' He placed his free hand under her chin and started to pull her face towards his, slowly, agonisingly slowly. 'I wanted to kiss you from that very first moment.' His lips were millimetres away.

'You scumbag, you maggot…' Alisha grabbed her phone from the desk and pressed decline hastily.

'Sorry about that,' she said and clicked it on to silent without looking and placed it back onto the desk before taking up the exact position they had held moments ago.

'Now where were we?' he asked, smiling slightly at her choice of ring tone.

'Something about wanting to kiss me.' She could hear her phone vibrating noisily as it rang again.

'Do you think you should get that?' His mouth was still hovering above hers.

'No, it won't be important.' She pushed herself even closer to him, her lips catching his slightly as she spoke. 'Everyone thinks I'm at home.'

'Everyone thinks I'm at home too,' he replied and smiled before finally claiming her lips. His hands wrapped around her back and pulled her into his embrace, her body moulding itself naturally to his as if they were made of one piece that had been chiselled apart. 'My parents are going to kill me.' He said before kissing her once more.

'Why?' She didn't really want to talk but felt he had more to say.

'I haven't told them yet.' He spoke between kisses. 'Is it ok if we keep this our little secret for a while?' His mouth had moved down her neck now and she found her hands starting to undo the buttons on his shirt. 'Just for a week or two.' He pulled her top over her head as she reached for the belt on his trousers.

'Just for a week or two,' she agreed as he pushed her gently back on to the desk and started kissing her stomach.

'Hands where we can see them!' Tom spun round and Alisha stared at the doorway to find two police officers standing there. 'Move slowly down on your knees with your hands on your head.'

'Officer please,' Alisha started to explain, grabbing her top to cover her modesty then dropping it instantly when the officer shouted hands where we can see them once again. 'I'm Alisha Jones, I work here, and my grandpa owns the place.'

'Sorry, Miss, but we've had reports of a break-in.' The two officers approached the now kneeling Alisha and Tom and started to cuff them, placing their hands behind their backs. 'You'll both be accompanying us to the station for further questioning.' One of the officers started to talk into his radio.

'Did you leave the shutters open?' she whispered to Tom who nodded apologetically. 'I've got ID in my bag if you'll just let me get it.' Alisha tried the second police officer this time, but the result was the same.

'On your feet.' The one who had been talking on the radio helped Alisha stand up as the other officer did the same with Tom and they started to lead them out of the office and down the stairs.

'Will you at least let us get dressed first?' Tom begged. 'You can't make her go outside like that; it isn't decent.'

'Wait there!' The second officer ordered and went back to fetch Alisha's top. The noise of feet running up the stairs made Alisha look first at Tom and then towards the rapidly approaching footsteps.

'So much for keeping it a secret!' she said sheepishly as she looked into the horrified eyes of her grandpa, Uncle John and of course, Marsha.

Chapter 14

'You can't sack me.' Alisha was trying not to shout, but she was having a hard time controlling her temper.

'I can sack you and I will.' It was now Friday and after being given the silent treatment since Monday, her grandpa was now in full attack and defence mode. 'You've brought this factory into disrepute and the name of Frosts has been associated with a scandal. Mr and Mrs Walker are mortified and if the contract hadn't been signed and sealed…well it doesn't bear thinking about.'

'Grandpa please…' Alisha begged. 'It's the twenty first century not Victorian times.'

'I don't care if it's the fiftieth century.' He blasted and thumped his fist on the desk. 'I will not have a granddaughter of mine cavorting around like she's some common trollop.' He quietened suddenly. 'How many times have you met him? Once, twice? Yet after not even being on a date with him, you're…you're…well I can't even say it.'

'Kissing him!' Alisha felt the fire raging inside her, all the years of pent-up frustration at her grandpa and his out-of-date ideals. 'That's all we were doing Grandpa…kissing!'

'Don't take that insolent tone with me Juliet, you're not too old to be slung over my knee and taught a lesson, you know.' He sat down in his chair. 'Your brother understands these things, so why can't you? He's found a wonderful girl in Marcie, but you…well, that husband of yours will never amount to anything, mark my words. I never wanted you to marry him, but your mother insisted and here we are no more than five years later, two kids down and another on the way and all you do is ask for money from me.' He looked up at her, a look of absolute confusion on his face.

'Are you ok, Grandpa?' Alisha made a step towards him. Juliet? That was her mum's name. Why had he been talking about her mum and dad and Uncle John and Marcie?

'Of course I'm ok.' He picked up his phone and asked Marsha to come in, she was there in seconds and Alisha suspected she had been waiting just outside the door. 'Please escort this young lady from the premises.'

'Grandpa!' Alisha cried once more. 'This isn't funny anymore. You've had your joke now let me get back to work.'

'I can assure you Alisha, this is no joke.' Marsha turned to look at her. 'I didn't want to be the one to say this, but it isn't just the incident on Monday.' She paused and looked over as if awaiting permission from the man at the desk that had aged ten years in ten minutes. 'Money is missing from the wages.' Alisha went to open her mouth, but Marsha shook her head. 'We are suspending you pending further investigation.' She took hold of Alisha's arm, and despite her protests, ushered her out of the office. 'For your own sake Alisha, just go quietly.'

Outside the door were Uncle John, Alison, and Alistair, all with solemn and disbelieving looks on their faces.

'I haven't done anything,' she protested, unable to believe the turn of events.

'You are not permitted to talk to anyone in this firm.' Marsha spoke as if she was a police officer reading the riot act. 'You are to collect any personal belongings and leave the premises immediately. All company property must be returned by the end of today and you are not to set foot on the premises until all investigations have been concluded.'

'You're really enjoying this, aren't you?' Alisha hissed under her breath as she was frog marched downstairs and made to clear out her desk.

'Believe me Alisha, this gives me little pleasure.' And for once, Alisha actually believed her.

'I can't believe it.' Lizzie was horrified as Alisha retold the day's events at the urgently called meeting at their local pub. Renee had made a few comments, having borne witness to Alisha's walk of shame through the factory.

'You shouldn't be here.' Alisha had warned Renee when she had turned up. 'I'm not supposed to talk to anyone in the firm.'

'I really don't give a monkey's arse,' she had replied, hugging Alisha till it hurt. 'That Marsha had no right.'

'I think she was the only one who could,' Alisha had said, surprising even herself at her defence of Marsha.

'I'll see what can be done from a legal point of view.' Fay started taking notes in her ever-present notebook. 'As you haven't actually been sacked, I don't think there is anything tribunal wise that can be done as yet, but I can certainly start building a case.'

'I hope it doesn't come to that,' Alisha was still in shock about it all.

'And what have your family said on the matter?' Lizzie asked. 'Surely they don't believe it?'

'I haven't heard from any of them,' she hung her head.

'Shame on them,' Fay condemned. 'How dare they?'

'It's not their fault.' Alisha could see her family's point of view. 'What Grandpa says goes.'

'Don't you dare defend them?' Renee scolded. 'I've a good mine to hand my notice in.'

'You will not!' Alisha declared. 'I won't have anyone losing their job because of me.'

'I agree with Lishe.' Lizzie stated, receiving surprised looks from Fay and Renee. 'I'm serious. Listen…we need someone on the inside.' It took a few seconds for what she was saying to sink in with the others. 'I mean, I can't believe we have to do this, but we have to prove Alisha's innocence.'

'What I don't understand.' Renee began. 'Is all that blustering about what happened with Tom? Do you think it was a cover or something? A way for your grandpa to let off steam?'

'He was proper angry Renee,' Alisha recalled. 'I've never seen him like it and then he went all weird and started talking to me as if I was my mum…well I just, I just don't know.'

'And speaking of Tom…' Lizzie teased.

'I haven't heard from him since the police released us on Monday.' Alisha shook her head as she remembered. 'I've never been so embarrassed in my life. I doubt he'll have anything to do with me after he hears about this.'

'Then he's a fool and not the man we first thought him to be.' Fay placed a consoling arm around her shoulders. 'Now let's get pissed and plot our revenge.'

Saturday dawned bright and beautiful and after a sleepless night, Alisha decided to take herself for a walk in Hartshill Hayes Country Park to clear her head and get her thinking straight. Facebook had been cruel to her that morning, shoving memories of her family under her nose as soon as she had opened it earlier. It would certainly be a very blue Christmas this year if the situation didn't get sorted, and soon.

Her head was throbbing from the numerous bottles of wine that had been consumed the previous evening and not for the first time in her life she thanked her lucky stars for such wonderful friends.

She knew she couldn't drive to the park so hopped on the bus and enjoyed a trip down memory lane thinking of the many times that she and the girls had travelled into town or into Coventry, ogling boys, shopping, and making £5 last an entire day.

The park was already busy with early morning dog walkers, and she headed off to the sunnier side to enjoy the warm spring sunshine. She'd always loved this place, even though she hadn't lived as close as she did now, it had often been a family favourite to visit on a Sunday afternoon.

Thinking of her family started to upset her so she pushed the thoughts out of her brain. Her mother had sent her an awful text after she had been told the news but thankfully her father had been far more supportive and the only one to openly say he didn't believe a word of it, but as he wasn't a Frost by blood, she knew he had nothing to lose and was always happy to go against the family.

It wasn't long before she came across her favourite tree, a huge Oak that had stood for hundreds of years. She often wondered about the stories this tree could tell and the things it had seen. She looked up into its branches and there, nestled in a small knot, was a stone, beautifully decorated with a unicorn and the word #islastones.

Turning it over, she found the words find, post, re-hide and after searching Facebook and Twitter, discovered the story of a local girl from Hinckley called Isla Tansey who had lost her battle with cancer. She had wanted to spread awareness of her condition, DIPG and asked people to paint and hide stones all around the world, taking selfies and re-hiding once found. She wanted to be famous and travel the world through her stones.

Alisha took a picture and posted it to Facebook, feeling humbled and inspired by the little girl's story and the bravery of her and her family. She took the stone with her and vowed to re-hide it somewhere special.

Chapter 15

It was May and Alisha had really had enough. The only member of her family that was talking to her was her father. Every time she went near her parent's house, her mother would stand at the doorway; her arms folded like some old-fashioned school ma'am. If Alisha tried to speak, her mother would shove her nose in the air and turn her face to one side. Although she'd never been close to her mother, it still made her sad to think that her own flesh and blood could believe her capable of stealing.

Renee was doing her best to investigate under cover but as she was a shop floor supervisor, it was very hard for her to keep making excuses to visit the offices and her frequent trips to the stationery cupboard next door to Alisha's office was beginning to arouse suspicion.

'I don't know what else to do?' she cried to Alisha after popping by on her way home from work. 'I haven't heard anything from anybody. They must think I've got a problem with the amount of pens I keep using. Honestly, I'm up and down those stairs like a yo-yo but it's like you never existed.'

'Never existed?' Alisha was shocked. 'I was only suspended; how can I not exist? What's happened?'

'Your desk has gone!' Renee exclaimed. 'Your name's been taken off the door, oh Alisha it's just awful,' she sobbed.

'There's a cloud hanging over the place. Your Grandpa walks round snapping at everyone. Mr Frost is miserable. Alison and Alistair can't string a sentence together and even Marsha has a face like a wet weekend. Honestly Alisha, everyone has remarked on the change in the place.'

'I can't do anything.' Alisha threw her hands in the air. 'I've been expecting a phone call at least, but it's been weeks and nothing. Surely they can't just expect me to roll over and take it? It's not just my job, they're my family.'

'It's downright criminal.' Renee consoled. 'You said yourself the new software was a nightmare, surely, it's just a clerical error somewhere. Why won't they let you find it?'

'Your guess is as good as mine.'

Fay wasn't having much luck either. As Alisha was receiving full pay and nothing official had been filed against her, she was finding it virtually impossible to implement any legal stance against the company. The only thing she could think of was a possible case for slander, but Alisha didn't want her family dragged through the mud, so Fay had agreed to let it go and hold fire until something official happened.

'You scumbag, you maggot…' Picking up her phone, Alisha made a mental note to change her ringtone at the earliest opportunity.

'You coming to the fair Lishe?' It was Lizzie.

'I can't face it, not at the moment.' She caught sight of herself in the mirror. 'I look a right state.'

'Then get in the shower.' Lizzie wasn't taking no for an answer. 'Because Fay is coming to pick you up. She'll be there in twenty minutes.' And with that, she put the phone down.

'Best do as I'm told then.' She headed upstairs, jumped in the shower and bang on twenty minutes later, greeted Fay at the door dressed in jeans and a baggy jumper, her soaking wet hair tied up in a bun.

'Make up?' Fay queried, noticing the large bags under her eyes and exceptionally pale face.

'Back seat of the car job.' Alisha held up her pocket mirror and cosmetic bag.

'Good girl.'

It was around a fifteen-minute drive to the fair by The Pingles sports centre. The girls had been going every year for as long as they could remember. Jimmy squeezed his mini into a tiny little space before backing out again and ushering Fay and Alisha out when he realised they couldn't actually open any doors.

The smell of freshly cooked doughnuts and candyfloss hit them as soon as they stepped onto the field and a screaming Lizzie and Renee assaulted them on sight with a far more subdued and polite greeting from David and Paul.

'I'm so glad you came, Lishe.' Lizzie linked her arm through Paul's and then through Alisha's on the other side.

'Didn't really have a choice, did I?' she replied, giving her friend a soft withering look.

'No, you're right, you didn't.' She squeezed Alisha's arm then dragged her and Paul over to the hook a duck stall.

Two hours later and with arms full of teddies and random toys, they decided to head to the local pub for a carvery. The Cedar Tree was just a five-minute walk away and after throwing the teddies into Jimmy's Mini, which now looked like a fairground stall all on its own with bear faces pressed up against the windows and a bow and arrow set lying along the parcel shelf of the boot.

'Alisha?' She turned at her name.

'Jason?' Of all the people she expected to bump into, it wasn't him.' Lizzie, Renee, and Fay immediately formed a protective barrier around her. 'It's ok,' she said to them, and they relaxed slightly but still looked like caged animals ready to pounce.

'Can we talk?' he asked. 'I think it's bloody awful what's happened.'

'You do?' Alisha was certain he would have sided with Marsha.

'Like I said, can we talk?' he asked again, and she nodded.

'You lot go on,' she spoke to the girls, who had no intention of leaving. 'I'll be fine.' They hesitated. 'I'll meet you there in a few minutes.' Reluctantly, they walked away, casting scowls over their shoulders as they went. 'Sorry about them.'

'It's fine.' He offered her his arm. 'They've every right to be angry with me. What I did to you was shit and what's happening to you now is doubly shit.' She placed her hand in the crook of his elbow and allowed him to lead her away from the car park and away from the fair.

'Where are we going?' she asked as they found themselves in amongst the caravans of the fairground owners.

'Marsha is here.' Alisha didn't need telling twice. 'I can't risk being seen with you, well any girl to be honest, she's so suspicious all the time.'

'Do you think you may bring that on yourself?' She couldn't believe she was defending Marsha Underwood.

'I don't suppose I help matters, do I?' he smiled, and Alisha's heart fluttered a little despite herself.

'See, there you go again, you can't help yourself.' She laughed and scolded at the same time.

'I only smiled,' he teased.

'But it's the way you smile.' She tried to explain, and they spent five minutes with each of them twisting their mouths into various smiles until they fell into fits of laughter.

'I've missed you.' He reached a hand up to smooth her hair and she knew he wanted to kiss her and for just a split second she would have let him, but the image of Tom's face floated into her mind.

'You said you wanted to talk.' This came out more harshly than she had imagined, more so at her own weakness rather than anger at Jason, but his hand dropped as if it was touching hot coal.

'Sorry, I shouldn't have done that.' He seemed to mentally dress himself down before beginning. 'Marsha was saying they are interviewing people next month to do the accounts and payroll.'

'They're what!' Alisha screamed, earning herself a look from a woman who had popped out of her caravan to hang the washing out.

'I knew you didn't know.' He hung his head. 'The world's gone mad.'

'Of course I didn't know.' She shouted in a hushed voice. 'How could I know? I'm not allowed to talk to anyone. My brother and sister don't talk to me, my grandfather has practically disowned me, and I think my mum would spit on me if she passed me on the street.' She shrugged her shoulders. 'What am I meant to do, Jason?'

'I honestly have no idea.' He rubbed her shoulders.

'How can I defend myself if no one will talk to me?' she sobbed. 'I just don't understand any of it. How can my family do this to me?' Jason's phone ringing interrupted them.

'It's Marsha, I'd better go.' He turned, then glanced back at her. 'Is your number the same?' She nodded. 'If I think of anything or hear anything, I'll text you.'

'Thanks, Jason.' She smiled as best she could and watched him disappear through the caravans.

How could they do this to her? Who was behind it all? Surely her grandfather didn't believe her capable of stealing.

Her brother? Her sister? Uncle John? It had to be Marsha; it could only be Marsha. An idea went off in her head like a match being struck. Marsha had implemented all the new systems, but it was Alisha that had to use them. Was this a smoke screen? Was this a way for Marsha to get rid of Alisha? Were Alistair and Alison next?

'Hello, dearie.' Alisha hadn't noticed that she had company. 'You look mighty troubled.'

'I know you.' She looked at the middle-aged woman, racking her brain for recollection. 'You're the lady from the Christmas ball.' It had been hard to recognise her at first as she didn't have the heavy make-up on, but Alisha would recognise those startling blue eyes anywhere.

'One and the same.' She inclined her head in greeting. 'So what are we going to talk about first, Alisha Jones? Your cranberry dream or this nonsense about you stealing money from your grandpa's company?'

Chapter 16

Alisha didn't know what she was more shocked by. The woman knowing her name or her troubles.

'Come on, dearie, you look like you could do with a nice cup of tea.' Mouth still wide open in shock, Alisha followed her to a caravan at the back of the field.

'You live here?' Alisha had expected a red and gold wooden caravan on huge cartwheels with a rather large shire horse to pull it. Instead, she found a beautifully modern caravan, gleaming white, with a neat clothesline hung up outside.

'What were you expecting?' Alisha shook her head and wouldn't answer, ashamed of herself for the stereotype imaging. 'We save the horse and carriage for special occasions.' The woman giggled and headed inside, beckoning Alisha to follow. 'Come on, dearie.'

'It's lovely,' Alisha exclaimed as she stepped inside. 'Do you live here on your own?'

'Goodness me, no.' She busied herself making tea and shooed Alisha to the table and chairs that sat in the middle of the caravan. 'My husband runs the dodgems with the help of our two sons. Both married themselves now with kiddies on the way.' Alisha saw the look of pride on her face. 'Anyway, enough about me, Miss Jones, we're here to talk about you.'

'What's there to say?' She shrugged her shoulders and thanked her for the mug of tea as she sat down opposite her. 'I'm a failure. My family won't speak to me, and I turned my last boyfriend gay!' There were no tears left, she didn't seem to be angry anymore, just resigned to her fate.

'Let's start with your family then.' And Alisha found herself telling the whole sorrowful tale, even the part about Marsha being 'sacked' from Dunnings. 'Seems to me, my lovely, that you need to grow a backbone.'

'But I tried that.' Alisha whined remembering that awful Friday morning in her grandpa's office.

'Have you?' The woman's blue eyes seemed to be piercing her very soul. 'Looks to me is that all you've done is a lot of whinging and moaning about doing stuff and not an awful lot of actually doing stuff.'

'Err…well…but…' Alisha spluttered before realising she was completely and utterly correct.

'Well at least we've got that sorted.' Alisha wasn't sure what they had got sorted and was about to ask when the woman continued. 'So, the dream.'

'I don't understand any of it.' She was hoping for some kind of clarification.

'Well, you're not meant to understand it.' Alisha's face must have said it all because the woman laughed. 'It's a dream dearie, make of it what you will.'

'But you said it would show me my future husband!' Alisha protested, feeling slightly misled.

'And so it did.' Alisha was getting confused now.

'You just said it was a dream.'

'Dreams can mean everything, or they can mean nothing.' Alisha rubbed her temples. 'They can show the past, present, or future. They can tell us our deepest, most hidden thoughts or just random pictures as our brain sorts through the day's memories.'

'Well that's about as clear as mud.' Alisha finished her cup of tea.

'What did you see?' She picked up Alisha's mug and started swirling the dregs around in the bottom before tipping the last bit of liquid out onto a plate that was sitting on the table.

'A big fat cranberry covered in frost that burst to reveal a wedding ring.' Alisha gave the shortened version.

'And which part of that exactly is confusing you?' She was staring into the bottom of the mug and nodding.

'Erm…all of it.' Alisha resisted the urge to get up and peer into the mug over the woman's shoulder.

'I shall explain one part of it for you.' She put the mug down, a satisfied look on her face. 'Your choice.'

'One part?' The woman nodded. 'But…'

'One part,' she repeated. 'The leaves have explained it further to me but too much information can change your path.' Alisha racked her brain, which bit was she most intrigued by?

'The cranberry,' she said after a few seconds.

'Really?' The woman seemed shocked. 'You want me to explain the cranberry?' She shrugged her shoulders. 'It's a name.'

'That's it? A name?' Alisha wished she'd asked something else. 'But whose name? My future husband?' If that was true, then Tom was out the window, as well as every single man she knew. 'But I've never met anyone called Cranberry.'

'Why don't you take another potion.' She stood up and handed Alisha the exact same muslin bag that she had given her at the Christmas ball. 'This time sprinkle it in a glass of warm red wine on Midsummers Eve. Concentrate on your dream, look at everything.'

'Alisha?' It was Lizzie's voice.

'Alisha?' This was Fay's, followed by Renee.

'Your friends are looking for you.' The woman folded Alisha's fingers around the bag. 'Love is the world's most powerful creation.'

'Thank you,' she said, smiling as she headed to the door. 'I'm here.' She walked down the steps, slightly startled that it was starting to get dark.

'Where have you been?' The three girls scolded in unison.

'We've been worried sick.' Renee waved her phone. 'What's the point of this if you don't answer it?'

'I'm so sorry.' Alisha pulled out her phone. 'Battery must have died.'

'Alisha!' Fay screamed. 'What if something had happened to you? Why can't you keep your phone charged like normal people?'

'Because I forget.' She couldn't believe she'd caused her friends so much worry.

'It's a good job we saw Jason, or we'd never have found you.' Renee hugged her.

'He came up to Paul in the toilet and started talking to him.' Lizzie was laughing now, relief etched on her face. 'Paul had no idea who he was, and it was only when he mentioned your name that he realised it wasn't a come on.' Lizzie laughed again.

'So what were you doing there?' Fay inclined her head towards the caravan.

'It was the fairground woman from Christmas.' Alisha filled them in on the way back to the car park.

'Why didn't you ask about the empty plate?' Fay chided.

'I'd have asked about the table being laid for one,' Renee commented.

'Or why it burst.'

'Alright, I get it, I know I asked the wrong question.' Alisha squashed herself into the back of Jimmy's Mini along with the teddies and toys.

'Did she say anything else?' Fay asked as they drove out of the car park, waving at the others who were getting into David's car.

'No.' Alisha squeezed the little bag in her hand. 'Nothing at all.'

Chapter 17

Alisha awoke the next morning full of positivity and renewed optimism. She sat at her dining room table with a notepad and pen and scribbled down her plan of action. Could she say all these things? Dare she say all these things? Would she even be able to get past the door at Frosts? But then the fairground woman's words rang in her head, and she stopped doubting. She wished it was a workday and not Sunday because she would have been on her way to the factory right now to say her piece and demand not only her job back but her place in the family.

Just one more day and one more sleep to get through and then she would be up with the lark and waiting on the front step when Uncle John came to open up. It was always Uncle John that opened up, unless he was on holiday and then either Alison, Alistair or Alisha would do it.

She knew Uncle John would let her in, well she hoped Uncle John would let her in. Out of her and her siblings, she was the closest to him. The three Jones children were treated almost like John and Marcie's own children, something which never went unnoticed by Alisha's mum. She could remember one Christmas when she was eight and her mum had told her off that she'd wished Aunt Marcie could have been her mum and this was probably the one and only time her mum had been lost for words.

Of course, she didn't really wish Aunt Marcie was her mum, but her mum was such a strange creature. Nothing like Uncle John and certainly nothing like her gentle and caring grandmother. If anything, she was like Grandpa Frost, but whereas he channelled his strictness and sharpness into work, her mother focused it on her children and husband.

She never really knew why her mum and dad were still together or even how such a soft man as her father had fallen in love with such a harsh woman. 'She was so different when she was younger' was all he used to say when asked, and no amount of questioning would induce any further answers.

Alisha spent a few hours writing, crossing out and quite often re-writing what she wanted to say and by lunch time was satisfied that she had enough down on paper and in her head that she wouldn't get tongue tied or suffer a complete memory blank in front of her grandpa.

Nerves suddenly overcame her as she thought of her grandpa. What had happened to him lately? He'd always been stern with them, Alisha in particular, but she remembered many a time coming into the factory when she was little and being lifted on his shoulders for a tour of the different departments.

On one such occasion, they had gone to see the baubles being made, this was and still remained Alisha's favourite thing that the Frost factory made. There was something about the delicate beauty of them that just made Alisha smile. It had been the first time her grandpa had allowed her to hold one. It was silver with a snowman painted on one side and she had beamed from ear to ear as it twinkled in the factory lights. Then she had dropped it and it had smashed into a thousand pieces and she had cried. But instead of scolding, her grandpa picked her up and placed another one in her hand.

'One day, this will all be yours.' He had said, and she had wanted nothing more than to work in his factory for the rest of her life.

She knew that Alison and Alistair didn't feel the same. That they had just felt pressurised to go into the family business, and in a way, she respected her mum for going against the wishes of Grandpa Frost and doing her own thing.

Her stomach rumbled, and she realised that she hadn't eaten a thing all day. She'd been so preoccupied with getting everything written down that she'd forgotten to eat. As usual, there was very little in the cupboards and only some mouldy cheese and a piece of extremely limp celery in the fridge, so she decided to get in the car and head off to the local supermarket.

She drove to the retail park that was a few miles away. Chiquitos had opened a new restaurant there, and she thought she would treat herself to some fajitas before a bit of retail therapy and then the supermarket on the way home. That should kill a few hours, she thought to herself, put Free radio on the car stereo and sang along to the latest hits.

Pulling the car into a space, she stepped out and memorised the letter on the sign nearest. This car park was well known for people forgetting where they'd parked, and shoppers quite often walked up and down the rows searching desperately.

Alisha was used to eating on her own but was grateful that the waitress sat her on a table, that was virtually hidden behind a large pillar. It was a popular restaurant, and she really didn't want to see anyone she knew.

Four stuffed tortillas and a slab of vanilla cheesecake later and Alisha was feeling full and satisfied. She paid the bill, left a tip for the waitress on the table, and then headed over to the supermarket. She passed the large department store on the way, stopped to look at the extremely comfortable looking sofa that was in the window and then did a double take as she watched Tom walk past in front of the window and sit in one of the chairs on display.

She was in two minds as to whether to go in and speak to him, but then she saw a brown-haired woman sitting in the chair next to him and from their body language, it was clear they were more than friends.

So he'd lied to her.

This was obviously Katie, the woman he was engaged to. But why were they over here? It didn't matter anyway, she said to herself. She was clearly just a diversion to pass some time, maybe sow a few wild oats before he settled down with Katie. How could she have been so stupid?

Just as she was about to move away from the window, Tom looked up and caught her eye. She had nowhere to hide as he raised a hand up and waved at her. She watched as he said something to the woman beside him, and then they both came outside.

'Alisha!' He seemed genuinely pleased to see her and even kissed her on the cheek. 'This is Katie. Katie, this is Alisha Jones.'

The woman held out a hand to Alisha and shook it warmly, a genuinely happy smile on her face. 'It is an absolute pleasure to meet you, Tom has told me so much about you.' She had an incredibly posh accent, every single word pronounced to perfection. 'We were just about to grab a coffee; would you care to join us?'

No, she would not care to join them, she wanted to say, but instead Alisha agreed and even nodded her head.

It was only a short distance to Starbucks; Tom was walking beside her and Katie was a few steps behind.

'I'm sorry I haven't called.' He held the door open for her as they stepped in.

'Oh. I completely forgot.' Katie paused just as she reached the door. 'I promised Mum and Dad I'd go over the guest list with them. My sisters are coming round too, so I can't not be there.' She placed a hand on Alisha's and squeezed it gently. 'It's been lovely to see you, I just wish it could have been longer.' She turned to Tom. 'Will you be ok getting home?'

He nodded. 'I'll grab a taxi or the bus.'

She blew him a kiss and then was gone, but Alisha had found herself rooted to the spot.

'Guest list,' she whispered to herself. 'Guest list!' She spoke much louder the second time and the couple who were seated near the door looked up at her. 'Wedding guest list? You're still getting married,' she accused.

'No, Katie and her family are organising an anniversary party. I told you I'd called it off, we just hadn't told our parents, but the little episode with the police kind of put paid to that.' He grinned as if remembering that night and Alisha couldn't help grinning with him. 'Honestly Alisha, I know I haven't done anything to make you trust me, but if you just give me five minutes, I'll explain everything.' She looked at him a little doubtfully. 'Please?'

The way he looked at her made her feel all wobbly inside.

'Five minutes,' she insisted. 'And you can buy the coffee.' She headed off to a table at the back of the shop and settled herself down whilst Tom bought two coffees, grabbed sugars and two wooden stirrers before joining her.

'How are you?' Alisha hadn't expected him to start with this question. She'd thought he'd maybe have opened with a full apology, but the way he asked and how he was looking at her with the most heartfelt sympathy in his eyes made her collapse into a heap of tears. 'Oh God, I didn't mean to make you cry, I'm so so sorry.' He shuffled his chair round so he was sitting next to her and placed an arm around her shoulders.

'I just don't know what to do.' She'd already started having doubts about the speech that she'd written. 'I haven't done anything wrong, but no one will believe me.' She sniffed into his shoulder. 'Why won't they believe me, Tom? They're my family. What makes your family turn on you like that?' She looked up at him.

He raised both eyebrows with a wry smile. 'From how my parents and Katie's have reacted to this, I'd say it's when you do something that they don't agree with.'

It was her turn to be sorry. 'Is it because of me?' He shook his head.

'No, it's because of me.' He pulled a tissue from his pocket and dabbed her eyes. 'I should have stood up to them years ago, but I just went along with the Katie thing, and it seemed to make them so happy, and I wasn't in love like I am now.'

Had she misheard? 'You're in love?' she asked.

'Totally and utterly,' he replied. 'From the very first moment I saw you.' He placed a finger under her chin and brought her mouth to his. 'I'm sorry I've kept away from you.' He started to explain after the small kiss had ended. 'It's just been an absolute nightmare with Mum and Katie's mum and then dad has been trying to find a way out of the merger.' Alisha's mouth dropped open in shock. 'Of course there isn't one, and I've told him it would be the end of us, and I think he's finally calmed down and come to terms with it. Mum, on the other hand.' He wiggled his outstretched hand. 'Mum I'm not so sure about.'

'It's such a mess, Tom.' She felt better for being around him, for being able to talk with him again and the news that he was in love with her hadn't hurt either.

'Then we need to sort it out.' He stroked her arm. 'Every last little bit of it.'

Chapter 18

It was starting to rain when they came out of Starbucks, so she offered him a lift home, which he politely declined, saying that it was all still fresh and raw for his parents and that if they saw them together, it might make things worse. So they sat in her car for a little while, holding hands and just talking.

'I want us to work, Alisha,' he said, and she knew he was speaking the truth. 'I'm not going to lie to you, it's going to be hard and there might be times we don't see each other for a while but we can text and call each other.'

'We can video chat.' Alisha quite liked this idea, at least she would be able to see his handsome face, but Tom shook his head.

'Dad doesn't allow the internet at home.' Alisha looked at him gobsmacked. 'He only allows it at work because he knows he has to, or the business won't move on.'

'But your dad seems so nice.' She realised as she spoke that this statement bore no resemblance to what Tom had just said.

'And because he doesn't like technology, that means he wouldn't be nice?' Tom gave her a quizzical smile.

'I realise now that it was a stupid statement.' She shook her head in disbelief at herself. 'Your dad really is nice though.' She looked up at him. 'And your mum.' She said this as an afterthought, and he laughed.

'Don't worry, I know Mum can be a bit of a stickler.' Alisha had only met Mary Walker the once so most of her opinion of her had been based on what she'd heard from others.

'My mum isn't the best either.' They had talked and talked, neither noticing the time, neither caring until Tom looked out of the window and realised that the car park was almost empty.

'Goodness me, is that the time?' He looked at his watch. 'It's almost five, look, everyone is leaving.'

'Are you sure I can't give you a lift?' she asked again. 'I could drop you a couple of streets away if you're worried about being seen.'

He thought for a few moments and then smiled and nodded. 'Go on then, it's about twenty minutes away from here and I'd rather spend those twenty minutes with you than in the back of a taxi.

'Here's fine,' he said as Alisha parked up in what was an extremely affluent area. The road was wide enough for four cars, there were hardly any parked on the street, probably because each house had sweeping drives, most with security gates and four or five cars parked on them.

'You live round here?' she gasped in awe.

'Just a few streets away.' He pointed forwards out of the windscreen. 'The Walkers have been here for generations.' He turned round and looked out of the back. 'In fact, that house just there.' Alisha followed his finger with her eyes.

'The one with the lions standing on pillars?' He nodded.

'My great grandfather built that with his two brothers for their parents.' He looked out of the side window. 'And that one there for himself and those two there as well. They all lived on this street.'

'That's amazing to have such history.' Alisha had always found family trees interesting; she'd traced hers back on one side to the 1600s but had got stuck then as the surname had become Smith. 'So why doesn't any of the family live here now?' She assumed this was the case as surely, he wouldn't want any of his family seeing them and reporting back.

He shrugged. 'Just moved on, I guess.' He turned in his seat. 'It's been so good spending time with you today. I'm so glad we bumped into each other.'

She turned to face him as well, this being a little more difficult with a steering wheel in the way. 'Me too. Is there any chance of us bumping into each other again anytime soon? You can come to mine whenever you like.' She realised this sounded brazen, but at that point in time she really didn't care. He liked her, she liked him, and that was all that mattered. Sod what his family thought.

'I'd like that.' His face lit up and Alisha knew she would like it too, really like it. 'Text me your address and I'll come over one night in the week if that's ok?'

'That would be more than ok.' She placed a hand on his thigh, as near to the top as she thought he would allow, and his sharp intake of breath was her instant reward. 'I want to see you more and see more of you.' She moved her hand to the inside of his thigh and knew he understood her completely.

It happened so fast that Alisha was initially taken by surprise, but the feel of Tom's lips on hers was enough to push all other thoughts aside. She matched his passion, kiss for kiss, touch for touch, until they were both breathless. A beeping phone made them pause briefly. They looked each other straight in the eye, both thinking the same then deciding that they really didn't care who it was and went straight back to kissing each other.

By now, Tom's shirt was undone, and he'd expertly unfastened her bra to give him easy access to her breasts which he was currently kissing and caressing. The beeping sound came again, and neither even paused, but when it turned to ringing, Tom stopped.

'I'd best get it.' He sat back in the seat with a sigh and Alisha did the same. 'Hi, Mum. Yeah, sorry I'm late, got talking to a friend. No, Katie isn't coming for tea. Yes, I'm almost home.' He looked at Alisha and she knew their little clinch was at an end so started to tidy her clothes back up. 'I'm sorry,' he said after clicking off the phone and starting to do his buttons back up.

'It's ok.' She placed a hand on his cheek. 'We've got all the time in the world.'

Alisha watched the sun rise the following morning, sitting in her swinging egg chair in the garden. There had been two reasons why she hadn't slept, one of them being Tom and the events of the previous afternoon and the other was the impending visit to Frosts. She'd tried to think about Tom more than the other one, but her brain wouldn't allow it and the more she focused on the kisses they had shared in her car the more her mind pushed it away and brought her family into the forefront instead.

But now, as the dark night gave way to a gorgeous, warm spring morning, she was able to bring the happy thoughts back. She couldn't wait to see him this week and hoped he would visit sooner rather than later. She had texted him her address as soon as she'd got home, and he'd replied with a bunch of kisses.

Good luck for today xx

She really hadn't expected him to text her, and the sight of his name on her screen made her go all strange inside.

Thank you xx

She replied, making sure to use the exact same amount of kisses that he had put.

I thought I might pop round later and you can tell me in person how it went xxx

Her heart sang.

Shall I cook us some tea? xxx

As long as I can have you for pudding xxxx

You can have me for starters, main and pudding if you like xxxx

She waited for his reply, but nothing came. Feeling somewhat disappointed, she headed back inside the house to make a cup of tea. For half an hour she checked her phone, but nothing came and just as she was about to get showered and dressed, there was a knock at the door. It was a little early for deliveries and anyway she wasn't expecting anything, so she peeked out of her front window, screamed with delight, and then ran to the front door, completely forgetting that all she had on was a little camisole nightie and no pants.

'You came.' She opened the door to find Tom standing there.

'Not yet!' he said, striding into the house and looking at her as if he would devour her where she was standing. 'But it's not going to be long.' He slammed the door behind him, throwing off his shirt as he went. Alisha stepped back into the living room, enjoying watching him take his clothes off.

His body was gorgeous. She could tell he didn't go to the gym, who had time for that anyway, but his arms were toned and his stomach flat with just the hint of hair whisping out of his boxer shorts which, Alisha noticed with a gulp, were now the only thing he was wearing.

'I was expecting you this evening.' She was so far in the room now that if she took one more step, she'd fall onto the sofa.

'I couldn't wait till this evening.' Alisha could tell by the bulge in his shorts that this was indeed true. 'I'm surprised I waited this long to be fair.' He took another step towards her. 'I haven't slept all night.'

'Neither have I.' She took another step back and managed to fall elegantly onto the sofa, he was instantly beside her.

'I want you so much.' He kissed her neck, her breasts, down her stomach and then lower. He gently pushed her legs apart to give himself better access, and just as she was about to come, he stopped. Although slightly disappointed, she soon realised why. 'I want us to come together the first time.' She nodded as he held the foil packet up in front of her and then ripped it open with his teeth.

The feel of him inside her was almost enough to push her over the edge and in the end, she came first, her moans causing him to thrust harder and follow her in his climax just a few moments later.

They lay together, not moving, just enjoying the feel of each other, the afterglow of sex was just as good for Alisha as the sex was and she coiled a leg round his back so he couldn't move.

'I think I'm in very real danger of falling in love with you, Mr Walker,' she said as he lifted himself up on one elbow to look at her.

'It's far too late for me, I'm afraid, Miss Jones.' He kissed her. 'I'm totally and utterly, mind, body and soul, in love with you.' Her heart flipped at his words. The rest of her life

might be falling apart, but at least she had Tom to keep her
going.

'You'd best show me how much you love me then.' Alisha
bit his shoulder. 'I'm going to need showing over and over
and over…'

He claimed her mouth before she could say anymore, and it
was almost noon before they even moved from the sofa.

'I thought you were going into the factory today?' he asked
as they shared croissants and coffee at the kitchen table.

'I was.' She dunked a bit of pastry in her cup, much to
Tom's disgust. 'But I'm having much more fun here.' She
picked up another croissant and placed one of the ends in her
coffee, watching Tom as she did. 'Won't you be missed at
work?'

'Almost definitely, but I really couldn't care less.' He
stepped out of his chair and moved over to her side, taking
the croissant out of her hand as he did. 'That it is a very dirty
habit you have Miss Jones and I think I may have to punish
you if you do it again.' He placed his hands on both sides of
her chair, so he was leaning over her.

'Whoops!' she said as she threw a bit of pastry into his
coffee. 'I did it again.' She squealed then as he scooped
some of the frothy milk from the latte and spread it on her
chest.

'Punishment it is then.' And Alisha thought it was the best
punishment she'd ever had.

Chapter 19

'Do you want me to come with you?' Tom asked as they spoke over the phone. 'I know you're perfectly capable of handling yourself, but maybe for a bit of moral support.'

'I'll be fine,' she replied, every part of her wanting him to be there but knowing that his presence would just rile her grandpa more.

'Good luck for tomorrow then.' He paused. 'I love you.'

'I love you too.' They had spent three days together, three glorious uncensored, uninterrupted days together where they hadn't answered one phone call or text, ordered food deliveries whenever they were hungry because Alisha still hadn't been to the supermarket and got to know each other intimately through talking and passion.

She sat down on the sofa and posted a chat in the girl's What's App group; Renee was the first to answer, and she spent the next thirty minutes once they had all joined filling them in on her week so far.

Fay then posted a photo of Stonehenge and the words 'guess where I am?'

Alisha had completely forgotten it was the summer solstice. She searched high and low for the pouch the traveller woman had given her and was relieved to find it in the pocket of the jeans she'd had on that day, grateful that she was appalling at chores and hadn't got round to washing them yet. There was always red wine in the house, so she grabbed a glass, sprinkled the contents on top and then gulped it down.

Then she had a bizarre thought that she had, on no less than two occasions now, basically taken drugs given to her by a stranger in the vague hope that she might dream about her future husband. How old was she? Twelve?

She hopped into bed, delighted but also sad that she didn't have to set her alarm anymore and hoped that after tomorrow she would have her job back, or at least her family.

The dream was the most bizarre one that Alisha had ever had. It flitted around so much that she couldn't remember most of it when she woke up, but the biggest thing that stuck in her head was that she was chasing a cranberry. The whole dream, all she was doing, was running after the red berry and never seeming to be able to catch it. One minute it was cold in the dream, then hot, another time it was raining and then the last thing she remembered is that it was Christmas and again she dreamed of it bursting and turning into a wedding ring.

'Well, now I'm even more confused than I was before,' she said to herself as she showered and dressed for her trip to the factory. She chose the most professional outfit that she owned, which only came out for important meetings with big clients or the accountants. It was a pencil skirt, mid-calf length in black of course with a tailored black jacket that sat neatly on her hips, and she matched it with a blue blouse.

A cheeky message from Tom on the car's Bluetooth system cheered her as she drove to the factory. It hadn't changed a bit, of course it hadn't, what did she expect? The whole factory to fall apart because she wasn't there.

It felt like coming home as she walked through the office entrance and straight up the stairs. The familiar smell of glue and paint and oil from the machines filled her senses and she breathed it in. She resisted the urge to look in on her siblings and uncle and instead went straight to her grandpa.

'Grandpa, I need a word with you.' She didn't even knock, just walked straight in. 'This can't continue any longer. I've done absolutely nothing wrong, and no one will listen...Mum!' The last person in the whole wide world she had expected to see in her grandpa's chair was her mother.

'Hello, Alisha.' She indicated to the chair in front of the desk. 'I'm so glad you're here.'

'But...' Alisha was totally and utterly off guard as she walked towards her mum and sat in the empty chair. 'What on earth are you doing here?'

'I do own a third of the company, you know.' Alisha looked at her dumbfounded. 'You look surprised.'

Surprised wasn't quite the word that Alisha would have used. Astonished was probably more like it. 'I didn't know that.'

'Apparently, your brother, sister and the whole damn factory didn't know it either.' She seemed more annoyed than usual, and Alisha wished she hadn't chosen today to come in.

'Is Grandpa, ok?' The fact that he wasn't sitting in his chair made this question a little unnecessary but as Alisha had been kept out of the loop, she had to ask.

'He is,' her mum assured. 'He's officially retired now though, so I've stepped in to sort out this whole blasted mess.'

'You have?' Alisha couldn't stop the disbelief in her voice. 'But you've never worked here before?'

'Why does everyone keep saying that?' She threw down the pen she had in her hand onto the table. 'I worked in this factory alongside your grandpa and uncle for years and years right up until your father and I had you three. I wanted to come back but your grandpa said no, a woman's place was in the home. Honestly, as if I couldn't have done both.'

'I never knew that, Mum.' Alisha was starting to see a different side of her mum.

'Because I didn't want anyone to know,' she said. 'So I pretended to dislike Christmas and then it became such a big thing that I started to believe it myself. When you three started school, I began a business degree through the Open University so I could come back and prove to my dad that I was more than capable of bringing up a family and holding down a job but then your father got sick, so I had to stay home.'

Alisha really couldn't believe what her mum was saying. 'But Dad has been well for years now.'

'He has and for years I've been working at a company out of town.'

'You've been what?' How hadn't she known, but then she asked herself how would she have known? She hadn't lived at home for years now, so the daily comings and goings of her mum were alien to her.

'And now I'm here.' She folded her hands onto the desk in front of her and looked Alisha straight in the eye. 'And I don't for one second believe all this rubbish about you stealing from the company.'

Alisha was flabbergasted. 'Then why the silent treatment and looking at me like I was a piece of shit every time I came to the house?'

'Because I needed to carry on the pretence.'

'I don't understand, Mum.' Alisha really didn't.

'There's something wrong with your grandpa, we're not sure what but he's changed recently.' Her mum heard her gasp. 'He's ok, really he is,' she soothed. 'But we've been trying to get him to the doctor, but the stubborn old goat kept refusing. Then he collapsed yesterday and now he's in hospital having tests.'

'Why didn't anyone tell me?' Alisha couldn't believe that no one had thought to inform her.

'Your dad and I came last night, but you were otherwise engaged, shall we say.' Alisha blushed. 'I hope Tom is treating you better than Jason did?'

'He is, Mum.' This still didn't excuse the lack of communication; he was still her grandpa, after all.

'We didn't want to tell you over the phone, so we were coming round again after work, but now you're here and now you know.' Juliet turned her computer screen towards Alisha. 'Something has gone seriously wrong here.' She pointed to the Revenue payments.

'I found that too.' Alisha edged her chair closer. 'I narrowed it down to the statutory payments but got sacked before I could find out more.'

'You haven't been sacked Alisha and once the share transfer goes through, you'll be equal junior partners with you brother and sister and be back in this office before you know it.'

'The share transfer?' Alisha's head was spinning from all the information. She'd come in, expecting a fight, and now she was being told her mum was running the place with her uncle and she was getting a share of the factory with her brother and sister. 'Who's shares?'

'Your grandpa's, of course.' She turned the screen back. 'Thirty three percent will be shared equally between you three and he's keeping one percent himself.'

'Does he know this?' Alisha couldn't believe Grandpa Frost would ever agree to this.

'Oh yes. He's signed the paperwork and everything.' Juliet smiled and placed a hand over Alisha's.

'How on earth did you manage that?' she asked.

'I think you mean who?' The door opened and Marsha walked in. 'It's so good to have you back Alisha.'

'Ok, now I'm totally and utterly confused.' Marsha was smiling and did seem genuinely pleased to see her.

'Marsha here is a business aide, she helps businesses implement new technologies and systems, brings them into the twenty first century.' Her mum was smiling again, and Alisha couldn't believe how much younger she looked. 'I met her at my other job and told her about Frosts.'

'I've never known anyone dig their heels in as much as your grandpa.' Marsha declared. 'But your uncle and I got there in the end and the paperwork has all been dealt with at the solicitors so it's just a matter of time now.'

'Do Alison and Alistair know about everything?' Alisha asked, annoyance starting to creep back in that they wouldn't tell their own sister.

'We've told them a little white lie I'm afraid,' Marsha informed. 'Said due to the formal police investigation they aren't allowed to contact you as it could jeopardise the case and end up with you being prosecuted for fraud.'

'Why would you tell them that?' Alisha's head was banging as she tried to keep track of the conversation.

'Because someone in this company has committed fraud Alisha, very, very serious fraud.' Her mum warned. 'We have to let the perpetrator continue to believe that you are taking the blame for it. They'll show their hand at some point.'

'And in the meantime, I have to just stay at home?' This was getting exasperating.

'Exactly,' Marsha concluded. 'The quicker you get out of here the better, I'll go and check that the coast is clear.'

'I want you to do some research at home, see if you can find anything out.' Juliet handed Alisha a small envelope. 'Put this in your bag and don't tell anyone you have it. It's a USB. When you get home, load it onto your work laptop, you can use my ID and password, so no one gets suspicious.'

'I can't believe this is happening.' Alisha placed the envelope in her bag.

'Now, did anyone see you?'

'I don't think so, but my car is in the car park.'

'When you leave, just look really upset and keep you head down just in case.'

'And don't talk to anyone either, not even Renee if you see her.'

'Jesus Christ, is it really that bad?'

'Yes, Alisha, it is.' Her mum kissed her on the cheek and walked her to the door. 'And don't come back again, you're no daughter of mine.' Juliet shouted and winked at Alisha as she hurried down the stairs. She heard the door slam and was just on the bottom step when she heard the other office doors opening and the voices of her siblings. As ordered, she kept her head down and ran straight to her car, her mind reeling from all that she had learnt that day.

Chapter 20

Alisha was unsure how she had even managed to get home. It was one of those drives where you're on automatic pilot. One minute you're driving and the next you're home and you don't really know how you got there. She sat in the car for what felt like hours as she tried to take in all the information she'd just discovered. The most worrying was her grandpa's health and the most surprising had been her mum.

She finally made it inside and switched on the kettle. She'd wanted to finish the wine from last night but had decided she was going to visit her grandpa that afternoon whether he wanted her to or not. Even though her mum had said he was ok, she couldn't bear it if something was to happen to him and these last few months were their last memories.

A frantic knocking and the sound of Renee's voice at the front door brought her out of her stupor.

'Don't you ever answer your phone?' Renee scolded, marching into the house, her work overcoat still on. 'I saw your car in the car park and then all hell broke loose. I took my lunch break early. What the fuck is going on?'

'Why didn't you tell me my mum was at the factory?' This fact seemed as much of a shock to Renee as it had been to Alisha.

'Your mum? At the factory? The Christmas Grinch?' Alisha knew she was telling the truth, in fact, Renee had never lied to her, and Alisha knew she never would.

'Not just at the factory, working there. Apparently, she's taking over from Grandpa.' Alisha was pacing around; she couldn't stand still.

'Well that's news to me and everyone else on the factory floor.' Renee sat down on the sofa with a plonk. 'What on earth is going on at that place? There's so many secrets and whispers. We've heard hide nor hair from the Walkers, we're meant to be sorting out the Christmas cake packaging with them next week. It's just all gone a bit Pete Tong, hasn't it? Alisha Jones will you bloody well sit down, you're making me dizzy.'

She did as she was told. 'Grandpa isn't well either.'

'We suspected as much.' Renee put a hand on her arm. 'But no one has been telling us anything and I didn't want to tell you something that was basically just idle gossip. We don't see any of the family anymore, they're all locked up in their offices. Your brother comes down now and again to bark orders, but we're generally just left alone. It's not the happy place it used to be.' Alisha ended up comforting Renee as she broke down into tears. 'I'm so sorry. I've been keeping it in for so long.'

'It's ok.' They hugged each other. 'I can't tell you much more but trust me when I say it's all going to work out. I promise.'

After Renee had left, Alisha got straight to work on the laptop. She poured over the payroll records for the past two years and by the early afternoon she was one hundred percent sure it was the maternity and paternity payments. There was something not right about the amount. In a workplace like Frosts, where everyone knew everyone, Alisha knew there hadn't been that many babies.

She looked at her phone to check the time and realised that she'd missed a call from Tom, she fired off a quick message to say that she would speak to him later and then headed off to the hospital.

As usual, it took her ages to find a space and when she eventually did, it was a little tight and she ended up scraping the side of her car on the wall. Then she had to ask which ward her grandpa was on so by the time she found him she was feeling considerably flustered and pissed off.

The sight that hit her made her forget everything though and she almost ran to the bed.

'Hi, Grandpa.' She held back her tears. He looked so frail and old, a shell of the man he had been when last, she'd seen him. 'It's me.'

'Alisha!' His eyes lit up, and he opened his arms. 'Where have you been? I wanted to tell you about the idea I've had for a new bauble.'

She hugged him tightly, sadness filling her because he felt like a bag of bones, how had this happened in a few weeks?

'How are you feeling, Grandpa?'

'I'd be feeling a lot better if they'd let me out of here, that's for sure.' He patted her hand as she sat down. 'Food is bloody awful.'

'Shall I go and get you some biscuits?' She could see that there was an empty packet on his table.

'Oh, yes please,' he smiled. 'And none of those blasted custard creams your grandma gets me, a nice shortbread or ginger nut.'

'I'll be back in a few minutes.' She kissed his cheek, relieved to find him happy and aimable without a hint of the past anger he had had towards her.

She popped into the little Marks and Spencer's and bought two packets of shortbread fingers and a bag of mini gingerbread men and grabbed some sandwiches whilst she was there and thought they could have a little picnic.

'Where the hell have you been?' Her grandpa shouted at her as soon as she got back on the ward.

'I went to the shop Grandpa, like I told you.' She started getting the things out of her bag.

'Spending my money again.' He sat up in his bed and wagged a finger at her. 'Left those children at home again have you with their bloody worthless father. Honestly, I don't know why you married him.'

'It's ok, Alisha.' She felt her grandma's arms go around her. 'Come away for a minute.' They sat down outside the ward.

'What's the matter with him, Grandma?' Alisha couldn't believe the change in him. 'He was fine a minute ago.'

'We think it's some form of dementia, I'm afraid.' Alisha put her hand to her mouth. 'I should have seen the signs, but I just kept telling myself it was his age; he's working too much, but when he collapsed yesterday, he didn't have a clue who anyone was. Kept asking where his mum was and when he could go home.'

'Oh Grandma.' She couldn't stop the tears from falling. 'Is it bad?'

'They've said he can go on tablets to help stop any further decline, but as you know with dementia, he won't get better but hopefully he won't get much worse.' Alisha couldn't believe how strong her grandma was being. She felt like her whole world was collapsing around her. 'Have you seen your mum?'

Alisha nodded. 'We've had a chat.'

'Oh I am glad,' she smiled. 'I've hated this whole thing, not being able to tell you about the investigation and then this with your grandpa. I just want to get him home and look after him and let you lot look after the factory as it should be.'

'I'm pretty sure I know what's happened.' Alisha knew her grandma had as much of a head for business as her grandpa did, she just chose not to use it. 'I just need to figure out how.'

'You get yourself home now and leave your grandpa to me.' They stood up.

'Can I say goodbye?' she asked.

'Let me see how he is.' Alisha nodded, not really understanding. 'You see, he changes when something else changes. He can be fine one minute and then if he goes out of the room or I go out of the room, it's like his brain flicks into a different part of his life.'

'Like a movie?' Alisha asked.

'That's a brilliant way to describe it,' her grandma remarked. 'The doctor said it's like he's living all these different times of his life, but his brain doesn't tell him which one is real anymore and if he moves out of one, he sometimes moves into another.'

'I just can't believe it,' she said as she watched her grandma poke her head onto the ward and then beckon for her.

'He's fallen asleep, give him a quick kiss and I'll give you a ring tomorrow to let you know when he's coming home.' Alisha walked onto the ward, left the biscuits on his table, and gave her grandpa a kiss on the cheek before wiping away tears that were threatening to spill over her eyelids.

'Don't give up Grandpa,' she said, squeezing his hand gently. 'Frosts never give up.'

The next few days past in a blur, she hardly left the laptop except to sleep. By Saturday she felt on the verge of success but after the computer crashed due to a thunderstorm and loss of power, she had to wait for it to reload and was so happy that after her previous run in with backups, all her work was indeed saved to the USB and also handwritten in various notebooks that were now strewn around.

'Look at the mess.' She started to tidy up, taking numerous cups and plates into the kitchen and then after catching sight of herself in the mirror above the fireplace she decided she needed a good shower and a break. She hadn't seen Tom or the girls in what seemed like forever, had totally neglected her phone and messages.

There was no answer from Tom when she phoned, and she hoped he would understand when she told him. The girls weren't answering either so as the rain had stopped, she decided to head off to one of her favourite places.

It was around a thirty-minute drive to Moorland Castle, although mostly a ruin, it still had a majestic gate tower which now housed a delightful tearoom and there was a sixteenth century church on the site which as was usual at this time of year, was currently housing a wedding. Alisha had dreamed of being married here when she was a little girl, and she couldn't help her thoughts wondering off to Tom.

It took her a few seconds to realise that it wasn't dream Tom she was seeing posing for a photograph. That it was actual real-life Tom, dressed in a bottle green tailcoat like the rest of the males in the group. That actual real-life Tom had his arm around the bride's waist and that the bride wasn't dream Alisha but the very real Katie.

Chapter 21

Absolutely nothing mattered to Alisha anymore. She couldn't care less about the factory, didn't give a stuff if people thought it was her that had committed fraud or if they didn't. She closed herself off from everyone and everything. Ignored her phone and all the front door knocks. Letters were left unopened and flower deliveries sent back to the florists. She had never felt so utterly low in her entire life.

Why had she believed Tom?

He'd clearly lied to her all this time, been lying to her from the moment they'd met. Pretending to be in love with her then buggering off the moment he got what he wanted. That wasn't strictly true, she admitted to herself. She'd been the one that had basically ignored him after they'd spent those glorious three days together, but to go off and marry someone else at the earliest opportunity? Well, that really was taking the biscuit.

She knew it hadn't just been a quick decision, weddings didn't get organised that quickly. No, he'd obviously lied the entire time, had never called the wedding off, had clearly never intended to either and the fact that he hadn't phoned or messaged or knocked at her door, showed that everything she thought was true. He didn't care for her and never had.

'Alisha Jones, will you open this bloody door right now or we are going to kick it in?' It was Lizzie. She had no intention of letting anyone in. She just wanted to sit on the sofa and feel wretched for the rest of her life.

'Right!' Fay's voice this time. 'Kick it in.'

Alisha laughed to herself, *as if they'd dare.*

The next thing she knew, there was crashing and bashing before her front door caved in and Jimmy and David stood there. Within seconds, her three best friends were inside.

'Fucking hell Lishe!' Lizzie went straight over to her whilst the other two started opening curtains and windows. 'What the hell is going on?'

Once there was light and fresh air in the house, the three of them sat down next to her and in front of her.

'It doesn't matter,' she shrugged.

'It clearly does matter, or you wouldn't be in such a state,' Fay piped in.

'We can't work out what's wrong.' Renee began. 'Mr Frost is out of hospital, he came to the factory the other day and Alisha, he looks so well. You've been cleared of all wrong doings, but no one has told us who did do it. Your mum is the best boss ever, and it's all sunshine and roses now, so what's going on?'

'Glad everyone is getting on without me,' she said sarcastically. 'That is so good to hear.'

'The Walkers are back as well.' Renee continued.

'Well it will be hunky dory again now Tom's gone and married Katie.'

'He's done what?' The three girls said in unison.

'Saw it with my own eyes.' She shrugged her shoulders as if it cared little to her what Tom had done. 'Bold as brass, at Moorland Church.'

'Surely not Alisha,' Fay commented. 'Are you sure it was Tom?'

'Of course, I'm sure.' She spoke angrily. I've had sex with the man, seen him naked, so I should know what he looks like in a bloody morning suit. More fool me for sleeping with him. Honestly, what is it with me and men lately? Do I have idiot tattooed across my forehead?'

'And it was a wedding?' Alisha, Fay, and Renee all looked at Lizzie.

'He was wearing a morning suit.' Alisha stated. 'Katie was in a wedding dress. They were kissing and having photos taken.'

'Are you sure it was Katie?'

'Does it matter?' Alisha couldn't believe they were asking such daft questions. 'He was getting married, had got married. He lied to me, end of story.'

'Well, if that's the case, then you need to pull yourself together and stop moping around.' Fay insisted. 'Shower and dressed and we're taking you out for lunch. Then this evening it's the summer ball.'

'I am not going to the summer ball.' She hadn't realised that it was tonight. 'No way in hell.'

'You are going, my girl, even if we have to drag you there by your hair.'

In the end, they didn't have to drag her. After many more tears and talks, Alisha had come back to almost her normal self and although they didn't make it out to lunch, by six thirty, they were all on their way to Christmas in July.

It was a strange feeling for Alisha. For the first time that she could remember, she was off to a Frost work party that she had had absolutely no part in whatsoever. The majority of the planning usually fell to her with a little help from Alison, but she had had no input on this one at all. In fact, this was probably the main reason she was going. She wanted to see who had planned it and if they were as good or even better than she was.

As soon as they arrived at the small hotel though, Alisha got her answer.

'Bloody hell!' Lizzie said, and not in a good way. 'What on earth is this crap?'

They stepped out of the taxis onto a white carpet which was obviously meant to mimic snow but was just a carpet and already grubby from people's shoes, so it looked more like grey slush. The usual majestic nutcrackers that they had at every Christmas event were missing, and there were tacky plastic snowmen instead.

Tinsel and baubles hung in the entrance hall of the hotel. Considering Frosts was full of these, whoever had decorated it had used the cheapest ones they could find, most looking like they were from the reject bin.

'This is just horrible.' Alisha couldn't bear to look and part of her wanted to run away, but curiosity got the better of her and they continued into the ballroom. 'For fuck's sake.'

There was probably only one thing that could have been worse than tacky, cheap decorations and that was no decorations at all. The tables didn't even have table covers on and everywhere Alisha looked, she could see disappointed faces. Frost events were well known for being extravagant, well planned, and thoroughly enjoyable. Alisha couldn't even see a DJ or any sign of food.

'Shall we just go home?' Renee asked, and Alisha could see a few people having the same idea.

'Not while Princess Christmas is here, no bloody way!' She hitched her dress up, tucking it slightly into her pants so it wouldn't get in the way. 'Fay, go and find me a manager. Renee, Jimmy, get to the factory and grab whatever you can so we can at least make these tables look half decent. David and Paul, please get rid of everything from outside, it just looks ridiculous.' She pulled out her phone and started making calls.

By eight o' clock the ballroom was looking vaguely decent, fish and chips had been delivered for everyone and Jimmy had downloaded a playlist that was currently blasting out of the hotel speakers. They'd somehow managed to whip up table decorations, and she'd even sourced a couple of bouncy castles to go outside in the grounds because she was never going to get a fairground here at such short notice.

'Not bad Princess Christmas, not bad at all.' Alistair's voice was behind her. Alisha turned to look at him, wanting to shout and scream at him, but instead she hugged him tight. 'I'm so sorry about everything.' He said. 'Mum said we couldn't talk to you, and we were so frightened that it would make things worse for you.'

'I know, Mum explained.' She hadn't really thought about that day at the factory since then. All her time had been consumed by Tom and the recent discovery that he was, in fact, a cheating liar with all the morals of an alley cat. In fact, that was an insult to alley cats she thought.

'Alisha.' It was Alison's turn now with a repeat performance and almost word for word explanation.

'Did you do this?' Alisha looked up in shock at her mum's voice. It was still alien to her to see her mum having anything to do with Frosts.

'I did,' her mum winked at her.

'Knew you would.' And then she grabbed the arm of her husband. 'Dance with me?'

'I thought you'd never ask,' her dad replied.

Alisha watched as her parents trotted off to the dance floor and started swaying together to the sound of, I Still Believe in You by Cliff Richard.

'This is really going to take some getting used to,' she said to her siblings as her dad kissed their mum on the cheek.

'The change in Mum is unreal,' Alistair commented. 'She smiles.'

'Never!' Alisha couldn't believe it.

'And sings,' Alison remarked. 'All the time.'

'Perhaps this was just what she needed then.' Alisha could feel the warm glow that used to be inside her starting to return and as the opening notes of Merry Christmas Everyone came over the speaker, she grabbed her brother and sister's hands and dragged them to the floor, their parents joining them.

She hadn't felt this good for a long time and although she knew there was many, many problems to solve and that there was going to be many bumps in the road along the way, as long as she had her family and friends travelling with her, she knew she'd be ok. She turned to give her friends a wave and a smile and it was then that she saw the biggest bump in the road.

Tom.

And not just Tom, the entire Walker clan, including the very new Mrs Walker looking absolutely stunning in a black trouser suit. Marsha and Jason had walked in with them, and Alisha got the feeling that something was going on, more secrets she thought, and she wished that just for once, she could enjoy herself.

She watched as Tom kissed Katie on the cheek and started to make his way over to her. She quickly looked for an exit and saw a door at the back of the room. She had absolutely no idea where it would lead, but at this moment in time she really didn't care. All she cared about was being as far away from Tom as she possibly could be.

'Alisha, wait.' He called after her as she picked her dress up and almost ran to the door, hoping that it wouldn't be locked, it wasn't. She wrenched it open and tried to close it quickly behind her, but Tom was too fast and had wedged his foot in between the door and its frame. 'We need to talk.'

She turned to face him as the door opened fully and he stepped in, allowing it to close behind him.

'Actually, Tom, I don't think we do need to talk.' She don't know what came over her, but she slapped him across the face. 'You've made a complete and utter fool out of me, pretending to love me, sleeping with me, lying to me and all the time you were making wedding plans.'

'It's not like that,' he pleaded.

'It looks very much like that to me.' She wanted to get away but as she made to find another way out, she realised that they were in a cupboard and a not very big one at that. 'Could you move, please?'

'Not until you listen to me.' He placed his whole body in front of the door.

'Tom, I have asked you to move.' She crossed her arms over her chest.

'I need you to listen to me.' He placed his hands gently on her arms. 'Please Alisha, I love you.'

'Then if you love me, you'll let me leave.' He looked at her with eyes full of sorrow and heartache but did as she asked and stepped away from the door.

Chapter 22

'What on earth was he thinking?' Alisha was back in work on Monday morning, and it felt wonderful, but talk with her siblings had inevitably fallen straight to Tom.

'They made no secret of the fact that they got married. Mr Walker told us and then apologised that we weren't invited but said there wasn't room.' Alison explained.

'There's one thing I don't understand though.' Alistair was biting his pen as he spoke. 'If they're all these big religious people, why wasn't it at their church? Why at a castle?'

'You don't listen, do you?' Alison scolded. 'The castle was just for photos. Honestly Alistair, you really need to pay more attention.' There was a pause. 'Are you ok, Alisha?'

Neither of them had realised that Alisha hadn't really joined in the conversation. She didn't want to talk about Tom or even think about Tom. She wanted to forget the whole sorry affair and try and get everything back to some semblance of normality. Due to the merger, she knew she was going to have to see him again at some point in the future, but hoped it was the distant future.

'I'll be giving him a piece of my mind when I see him next.' Alistair was looking at Alisha. 'The only reason I didn't lamp him one at the party was because there were too many people present.'

Alisha looked at her brother, he'd never so much as hit a fly in his life but she was glad of the sentiment all the same.

'Speaking of parties.' She wanted to change the subject. 'After the disaster that was Christmas in July, I'm going to start planning this year's Christmas ball. I want it bigger and brighter than ever before.'

'Oh that's a brilliant idea.' Alison agreed. 'Will keep your mind occupied and stop you thinking about other things.'

'But Christmas is months away.' Alistair moaned. 'I organised Saturday in a few days, and everyone said what a lovely time they'd had.'

Alisha and Alison laughed. 'Only because Alisha arrived to save the day. Honestly, Alistair, the decorations were abysmal, and you hadn't even organised any food.'

'Talking of food.' Alisha delved into her bag and handed a receipt to her sister. 'I believe this is your department. If you could ensure I'm recompensed for the fish and chips, I would be ever so grateful.'

The three of them were interrupted by Marsha's arrival. 'Tom and Mr Walker are here, they're in with Mrs Jones and Mr Frost at the moment but just thought I'd give you a heads-up, Alisha, in case you wanted to make yourself scarce.'

'Thanks, Marsha.' Those two words had never been uttered in the same sentence by Alisha before and as she stood up and started to make herself absent, she suddenly sat back down. 'Why should I?' She thumped her fists on the table. 'Why should I scurry away. I've done absolutely nothing wrong. He's the villain here not me. Running away like a frightened child. No, Sir. I've a good mind to march up there right now and give him a piece of my mind.'

'Perhaps off work premises might be a good idea.' Alison soothed. 'I know you're angry with him, but we do still have to work with them.'

'He is moving here, after all,' Alistair said nonchalantly.

'He's doing what now?' Alisha's mouth opened and she stared at her brother.

'Tom's going to be working out of here for a few weeks.' He looked at Alisha. 'You didn't know this?'

'Of course I didn't know this,' Alisha shouted. 'No one has spoken to me for weeks; how could I know this.' She pushed herself up off the desk. 'Over my dead body.' She barged past Marsha and stormed upstairs to what was now her mum's office. 'There is absolutely no way on earth that he is working here.'

'Alisha!' Where her mum should have been she found Renee and where she thought Mr Walker and Tom would be was a rather frightened looking young lad of sixteen.

'I am so sorry,' she smiled apologetically.

'This here is Billy.' The young man turned in his chair and waved hesitantly at Alisha. 'He's just applying for one of our apprenticeships.'

'So sorry.' She started backing out of the office. 'Lovely to meet you, Billy, you'll like working here. It's such a happy place.' She shot out of the door as quickly as she could, closing it carefully behind her before heading to her uncle's office, this time she knocked first.

'Come in Alisha.' Her mum's voice was calm.

'How did you know it was me?' she asked as she tried not to look at Tom and Mr Walker.

'I think the whole factory heard it was you.' She looked at Alisha from above her glasses. 'And before you say anything, Tom IS going to be working here.' Alisha went to protest, but her mum put her hand up to silence her. 'I suggest that the two of you head off somewhere for lunch and don't come back until you Alisha are capable of talking civilly to Tom.'

'But Mum…' Alisha whined.' He…'

'We all know very well what has happened Alisha.' Juliet folded her hands on her lap. 'But you are a shareholder of this company now and as such, that gives you certain responsibilities, one of which is working with Tom.'

'But why can't Alison or Alistair do it?' She still hadn't looked at either of the Walker men.

'I'd be happy to work with someone else, Mrs Jones,' Tom said, his voice almost apologetic in its tone. 'Perhaps Miss Jones feels incapable of the task.'

'Incapable!' *How dare he?* 'I am perfectly capable of any task Mr Walker, now if you'll give me five minutes, I will meet you downstairs and you can drive me to a VERY expensive restaurant, and I expect you to pay.' She stormed out of the room, closing the door loudly behind her. 'Not that a meal will make any difference, but if I have to listen to him at least I can have a nice lunch,' she said quietly to herself as she leaned on the door to regain her composure.

'Oh well played, Tom.' She heard her uncle say. 'Very well played.'

'If you're not going to speak to me, then why did you agree to come on this date with me?' The car journey had been completely silent on Alisha's part. As soon as she got in his car, she plugged in her Air Pods and looked out of the side window. She was absolutely determined to make him feel as uncomfortable as possible and she seemed to be succeeding. Now they were sitting at a secluded table in the garden of an Italian restaurant on the outskirts of town.

'Firstly, this is not a date. It's so far removed from a date that to call it a date is an insult to dates.' She was riled. 'Secondly, I am here for one reason and one reason only and that is because my mother has made me.' Not strictly true, she was there because he had insinuated that she was incapable, and she would never have anyone say that about her. 'And thirdly, I really, really want to know what you could possibly have to say to me that will make me think of you as anything other than a cheating arsehole.' There, she'd said it.

'It's not real.' Alisha went to leave. 'No, please, hear me out.' He begged, placing a hand on her arm, which she instantly snatched away.

'Are you or are you not married to Katie?' She could see him squirming. 'It's a simple question, Tom, you either are or you aren't.'

'Technically I am.' He lowered his head.

'Then there is nothing else to say.' She sat down in her chair, all hope that it had somehow been a joke faded away and she felt utterly done. 'I'll be civil to you at work, but nothing more.'

'It's in name only.'

'I really don't care, Tom.' She looked over at him. 'You lied to me. You made me fall in love with you, told me you weren't marrying her and then up and married her.'

'I did call it off, but then when I told my parents my dad went mad, he said if I didn't marry her, we'd lose everything.' He broke down in tears and Alisha just sat there.

'How can you not marrying someone mean you lose everything?' She was confused.

'The family are on the verge of bankruptcy, that's why we had to merge with Frosts to save the factory, but it still wasn't enough.' He took her hands in his. 'My dad was too nice, always too nice, he let people walk all over him. They paid themselves bonuses, pay rises, expensive cars, even holidays, all on the company.'

'But that's awful, Tom.' She could see now why her grandpa was as harsh as he was, if being like Mr Walker got you in debt. But surely there must be a happy medium?

'He borrowed money off the church years ago and then when it came to paying them back, he didn't have it.' He'd stopped crying now but his eyes were still shiny from the tears. 'He sold everything he could.'

'Don't tell me he sold you?' Alisha couldn't believe it.

'I was happy to do it, Alisha,' he pleaded. 'Katie is a lovely woman, she's kind, my parents like her, her parents like me, it seemed the right thing to do. People get married for worse reasons.'

'They also get married for better ones, like love.' She couldn't believe that in this day and age, marriages of convenience still took place.

'But I never thought I'd fall in love.' He said this with such honesty that Alisha believed him instantly. 'Then I met you.'

'And Katie knows all about this?' He nodded.

'I told her I'd met someone, explained everything and she was so understanding but when we told her parents and mine that we were calling it off her father went berserk, said the church would be a laughingstock, that he'd never be able to look his parishioners in the eye again.' Alisha really didn't like the sound of Katie's father.

'I still can't believe your parents and hers would force marriage on to their children.' He shook his head.

'In the end, they didn't.'

'You've lost me now.' Alisha was confused.

'In the end they said we didn't have to, but that's when Katie came up with a plan.' Tom sat back in his chair to allow the waiter to place two steaming plates of lasagne on the table in front of them. Alisha wasn't hungry in the slightest, but she picked up her fork and started to stab at the pasta.

'And what was this marvellous plan?' She placed a tiny piece in her mouth, it burned her tongue. 'Jesus, that's hot.'

'To get married, then get divorced, well, technically annulled.' Tom had eaten an even bigger piece of lasagne than Alisha had, and he had to spit it out. 'Bloody hell, have they cooked it in a furnace or something?'

'You've got some on your chin.' She handed him a napkin and he dabbed at his face, completely missing the sauce. 'Give it here.' She took the napkin from his hand and started wiping his chin. She couldn't help thinking back to Valentine's Day, when he had done the same for her.

'I've missed you.' He placed his hand on her arm, and she cupped his face with her palm.

'We can't just go back to normal, Tom.' She told him. 'I can't just forgive and forget. Whatever the reason was behind it, you still lied to me, and you didn't trust me enough to tell me.'

'But I did try to tell you.' His voice rose slightly. 'I texted you.'

'You bloody well didn't.' She sat back down on her chair and reached for her phone. 'Oh shit!'

Chapter 23

'You replied ok, talk later.' He reminded her. 'I thought that meant you understood what I was saying.'

'It still doesn't excuse it.' Alisha wasn't letting him wriggle out of it, even though she clearly hadn't read his message properly at the time.

'You put ok, talk later,' he repeated. 'Then I never heard from you, you didn't reply to my messages or calls. I even came to the house a few times, but I couldn't get hold of you and then it was too late.'

'I'm sorry, Tom.' He smiled at her and took her hand. 'But I'm only sorry that I didn't let you explain. I still don't think I would have been happy about it. What am I saying? I know I wouldn't have been happy about it.' She went back to her lasagne, which was now at the perfect temperature, and she discovered that she was ravenous.

Tom, on the other hand, seemed to have lost his appetite completely and was just pushing bits of pasta around his plate.

'I can't bear this Alisha.' His fork clattered onto the plate. 'You used to look at me with such passion and now you look at me as if you hate me.' He flung himself back in his chair.

She placed her fork down and looked at him over the table. 'I don't hate you, Tom; I could never hate you.' That wasn't true, up until a few moments ago she had thought she hated him. 'But what is there to do?' She shrugged her shoulders. 'You married someone else, there's simply no getting around it.' She held her hand up as he went to interrupt her. 'And I know you're about to tell me again about her family and you felt you had to marry Katie, but really Tom? Did you?'

'The whole ceremony I stood there, wishing it was you in front of me, wanting it to be you in front of me. I hoped someone would object, I nearly objected myself but in the end, I was too much of a coward. It was easier to go ahead with it by then than cause a scene by calling it off.' He sighed, his whole body seeming to deflate. 'What can I do to make it up to you?' He asked, and she knew he was being sincere.

'You don't need to do anything.' She wasn't sure there was anything he could do or if there was even anything she wanted him to do. 'We can at least be friends now.'

'But I don't want to be friends.' He was looking at her with such emotion in his eyes that Alisha almost crumbled.

'That's all I can offer you,' she spoke quietly. 'You broke my heart, Tom, and I'm not sure that you're the one to fix it.'

'I'm really sorry, Alisha.' He picked up his fork again. 'You honestly don't know how sorry.'

By the time the August bank holiday had arrived, Frosts was feeling like the family run factory it used to be. Juliet and John worked together so well that no one could understand why Mr Frost had stopped her working there all those years ago. The three Jones children were now back in the swing of things, and Christmas was well and truly in motion on the factory floor. Tom had been given a small office on the factory floor and spent his time between Frosts and Walkers.

He and Alisha were getting on well again. She'd always enjoyed his company, and they'd found an easy friendship after a couple of sticky first days.

'The coaches should be here in about five minutes.' Juliet, dressed in comfy travelling clothes, came bounding into the canteen where her three children and many members of staff were waiting around with various bags. Renee was busy doing her best trying to get people outside into the car park, but she was just being met with 'we will when the coach gets here' and in the end she gave up and came to stand with Alisha.

'I bloody well give up with them lot.' She said in exasperation. 'It's the same every year, they'll all rush out when the coaches come and there will be all this panic and commotion trying to get bags on board. And it will be all Renee this, Renee that.' She folded her arms across her chest. 'Well, I'm not doing it this year.'

'Ok, Renee.' Alisha knew that as soon as the coaches came, she and Renee would be the ones making sure everyone got on and that all the bags were in the hold.

'Is Tom getting on at Walkers?' Alisha shrugged her shoulders, ignoring the looks she was getting from everyone around her.

'He didn't say.' Alisha had tried to forget the fact that Tom and the Walker's staff would also be coming on the annual Frost summer outing. She actually didn't mind the staff, there was only around twenty of them, nothing compared to the size of the Frost contingence, and she was so glad that partners were never allowed on the trips as she didn't think she could face a weekend with Tom and Katie.

They didn't talk about Katie, or even anything about his home life. Alisha assumed he lived with her, you couldn't keep up a pretence of being married if you didn't live together and she tried not to think about whether they shared a bed. He'd insisted it was in name only, but surely, under the circumstances, he couldn't fail to be tempted. Katie was gorgeous, they made a beautiful couple, and Alisha knew that even if they weren't sleeping together at the moment, it was bound to happen in the future. This thought stabbed at her heart, and she pushed it away.

'The coaches are here!' Jimmy came rushing into the canteen, shouting. It was the same every year with him, he was like an excited schoolboy.

'Come on then you lot.' Alisha was grateful of the distraction from Tom, and as predicted her and Renee spent the next ten minutes ushering people into seats, making sure bags were on board and that no one was left in the factory. They head counted three times before nodding to each other that they were both happy and giving the drivers the go ahead to start.

'Every year Kelsey forgets something.' Renee said to Alisha as they sat down on the front seats.

'At least it was only her sunglasses this year.' She replied. 'Do you remember when she'd left her case in her dad's car when he'd dropped her off and then he'd gone off to work and she couldn't get hold of him.' They both giggled at the memory.

'We all lent her a bit of something, if I remember correctly.' Renee rested her head back on the seat. 'Walker's is basically on the way, right?'

'It's about a ten-minute detour, that's all.' Renee nodded and closed her eyes, so Alisha popped her pods in and settled down with Taylor Swift.

She must have nodded off because the next thing she knew she was jolted awake by the coach stopping and cheers from everyone as they waved at their new colleagues. The Walker's staff looked as if they were heading for an execution rather than a fun time away at the seaside, but Alisha could see how it must feel for them and was glad that most of them seemed to have turned up to at least give it a go.

'You stay here, I'll go and sort them out,' Alisha said to Renee.

The Walkers were far better behaved and more organised than the Frost crew and within five minutes they were all ready to go.

'Where's Tom?' Renee asked as Alisha got back on the coach. 'Isn't he coming?'

'Perhaps he's locking up.' She suggested, she hadn't seen him, and she really didn't want to admit to herself how disappointed she was going to be if he wasn't there.

'Shall I go and check?' Alisha shook her head.

'I'll go.' She stepped backwards off the coach.

'It's ok, I'm here.' As Alisha took the last step, she felt something hard and warm against her back. It was Tom. The smell of him was intoxicating, and she couldn't help taking in a deep breath. She felt his hands on her waist and was grateful for them because without them, she thought she might have fallen backwards.

'Everyone on board now?' The driver's voice brought her out of herself, and she realised she had been leaning into him and that his hands were still on her waist and somehow her head was tucked under his chin.

'Yes.' Her voice was higher pitched that normal. 'We're all ready to go.' She got back into her seat and Tom sat a few rows behind. She was glad that no one except the driver and Renee had seen their interaction, otherwise they would have been teased immensely.

The whole coach started to sing Summer Holiday as the driver pulled off and headed towards the motorway.

It was thankfully an uneventful and easy drive to the Somerset coast. Although the beaches weren't as sandy as Devon and Cornwall, Somerset was much closer to them and when driving on a coach, this was always a big issue.

Besides this, they'd been coming here for years now, always the same hotel and always the August Bank Holiday. Only COVID halted the annual outing and parties.

They pulled up to The Bucket and Spade Hotel, which sat right in the middle of the promenade. With the extra staff, they had actually filled the entire hotel for the first time and the owner, Jamie, came out to greet them as old friends.

'It's so wonderful to have you all back again.' He held out his hand to Alisha and then Alistair and Alison in turn. 'And you've brought the sun with you too, I can see.'

The weather was indeed smiling on them at the moment and Alisha hoped it would last for the entire two days.

'It's great to be back and thanks so much for fitting us all in.' Alistair and Alison had already gone to grab their bags, which left Alisha to check everyone in as always.

'I've got all our lot's details.' Tom was beside her.

'Jamie, this is Tom, he's joining us with his staff this year.' She introduced Tom and the two men shook hands.

'Pleasure to meet you, Tom, I hope you'll all enjoy your stay here.' Alisha and Tom followed Jamie inside and left the rabble to grab their bags and organise themselves. They always seemed far more capable of sorting themselves at the end destination than at the beginning. 'So we've got all the keys here, I haven't allocated any rooms specifically to people as I know you'll sort that between yourselves. Blue tags are double rooms, yellow tags are twins and red tags are singles. We've made as many of our doubles into twins, but I know you have a few couples in the group anyway.' Jamie handed her a whole bunch of keys. There were so many that Tom had to take some off her. 'We've put some tea and coffee making facilities in the breakfast room and laid on some sandwiches for you so you can head in there for as long as you need. Breakfast is between eight and ten and if everyone could fill in their choices for us tonight, that would be great.' He smiled at them.

'Thanks, Jamie.' From the level of noise that had suddenly emerged in the hallway of the hotel, Alisha knew that everyone was on their way, so she ushered them to the breakfast room. The sun was streaming in through the windows which had an unadulterated view of the sea, well, not the sea exactly as it was currently low tide but at least that meant it would be back late in the afternoon. 'Right then you lot.' Alisha called them all to attention after they'd all sat down and grabbed drinks and food. 'It's the same as every year but for our new guests, when I call your name, come, and get your key. You've already said what type of room you want so there shouldn't be any issues, but if there is just come and let me or Renee know.'

'Or me!' Tom put his hand up and everyone laughed.

After thirty minutes, everyone was happy and settling into their rooms. There had only been one change where a couple had split up since the booking and now wanted a room each. This had caused a little mess, but Renee had offered to share with Jenny as they were good friends anyway and Mike had taken the single that had been allocated to Marsha but as she'd been whisked away to New York by Jason, she now wasn't coming.

'Thank goodness for that.' Alisha took the two keys that were left off the table. 'Blue or red?' she asked Tom.

'You have the double,' he said. 'I'm fine with a single.'

'Are you sure?' She didn't like to admit that she was secretly pleased, she loved spreading out like a starfish in bed and hadn't slept in a single since she was a teenager.

'I'm sure.' He grabbed his bag. 'I'll see you later then.'

'Later.' She watched him head out and up the stairs, desperately wanting to say more to him but knowing that she couldn't. 'Ah well Alisha Jones, perhaps you'll meet the man of your dreams this weekend.' She took her case and bashed it up the stairs. 'Room twenty-four.' She read on the tag. It was on the second floor and at the front so she knew from experience that this would have an amazing view. She reached the end of the corridor, unlocked the door, and stepped inside. 'What the hell are you doing in my room?'

Chapter 24

'Your room?' Tom was lying on the double bed. 'This is my room, I thought they'd just made a mistake with the beds.' He sat up. 'Look.' He handed her his key. 'Room twenty-four.'

'But I'm in room twenty-four.' She felt like stamping her foot, but instead turned and tramped back down the stairs, Tom behind her. 'Jamie, there seems to have been a mistake with the rooms.' She explained the situation to the apologetic looking Jamie.

'I am so sorry, Alisha.' He started faffing with the computer. 'I don't really know how that's happened. They're shouldn't even be two keys for one room, except the staff keys.'

'It's fine Jamie, just find another room for me please.' Alisha watched Jamie as he lifted his head up from his computer screen and she could tell by his face exactly what he was going to say. 'You don't have another room, do you?' He shook his head. 'Well, we'll just have to ask everyone if they'll move.' She stormed off up the stairs with Tom hot on her heels.

'You can't do that,' he said, taking hold of her arm as she was about to knock on one of the rooms.

'Why ever not?' she asked, furious with the situation.

'Because everyone will be settled in now, probably unpacking and heading off.' As if to emphasise this point, one of the room doors opened and two of the employees came out already dressed for the beach.

'Hi Tom, Miss Jones.' They nodded their heads and Alisha was sure she heard whispering as they went down the stairs.

'Great!' She threw her hands up in exasperation. 'Now we'll be the topic of all the gossip.'

'Another reason to not go telling everyone then.' He started back up the stairs to the second floor and she reluctantly followed him. 'Would it be so bad to share a room with me?' He asked when they were in the room and the door closed.

Her heart and body were screaming no, but her head was yelling yes. 'But there's only one bed.' Her mind was remembering when they'd last shared a bed and it was giving her butterflies just to think about it.

'We've done it before.' He raised his eyebrows.

'You weren't married before.' Let him wriggle out of that one she thought.

'I'm not married now.' He was leaning on the dressing table that sat in the bay window. The sun was streaming in, and she could hear the gulls outside and the hustle and bustle of a busy seaside town. He turned to look at her.

'What do you mean, you're not married?' Her heart was skipping joyfully.

'We've applied for an annulment.' He was looking at her now with the most hopeful expression on his face. 'We applied for it almost as soon as we got married.'

'So technically, you are still married?' Her heart sank again.

'We're just waiting for the court to approve it. Then we'll just announce in a few months that we're getting divorced. I'm afraid I'm going to be the bad guy.' Alisha hated to think of him being known as the villain. 'I'll be thrown out of the church and my parents will have a hard time of it for a while.'

He was standing in front of her now. 'But that doesn't seem fair.'

'I don't care, Alisha.' He took her hands in his. 'I'd serve life in prison if it meant you'd smile at me again like you used to.'

'But you still kept it from me Tom.' Should she move on from the past? Could she let him in again?

And I can't change that, Alisha.' He squeezed her fingers softly. 'I wish I had a time machine. I wish I could go back but I can't. All I can do is promise you that I'll never hurt you again, that I will devote my life to our happiness.'

His words were making her waver and the sincerity in his voice and face were breaking her heart into thousands of tiny pieces. 'You broke my heart, Tom.'

'Then let me fix it?' His voice was pleading and as he reached in to kiss her, she didn't back away.

Just as their lips were about to touch. 'Don't keep anything from me ever again, Tom.'

'I won't.' He spoke softly, the end of the word lost as his lips claimed hers. 'I'm in love with you Alisha.' The soft kiss progressed quickly and before she knew what was happening he was naked from the waist up and her shirt was undone. She felt his hands move to unclip her bra and she stopped him. 'What's the matter?' he asked, confusion on his face.

'Let's take it slow.' She didn't want to give herself to him again, not so soon after being hurt. 'Can we just enjoying getting to know each other again?'

'Of course.' He started to do her buttons up, placing a kiss on her skin between each one until it was completely fastened, and he placed one last kiss on her lips. 'Whatever you want.'

Her phone started ringing, and she looked to see Renee's face smiling at her. She clicked it on to speaker.

'Come on slow coach, we're heading to the arcade.'

'I'll meet you there.' She switched off the call and turned to Tom. 'Let's keep the room share to ourselves as well.'

He nodded. 'Whatever you want to do, Alisha.'

The small group of Frost employees and Tom had spent the day in the arcade, walking along the promenade, eating ice cream and freshly cooked doughnuts, and then making sandcastles on the beach before the sea that had been miles away was all of a sudden covering all the sand. Everywhere they went, there was another group of Frost or Walker employees, and Alisha was happy to see that at least one group contained both.

Alisha had been glad of the company as it kept her and Tom apart and she needed some time to get her head around the whole situation. She'd confided in Renee during a toilet trip and Renee had advised her to go for it but had agreed with her on taking it slow.

'It's like having your first dates all over again.' Renee had said. 'You only normally get to do that once.'

Juliet and Alison had announced they were heading off to catch a show and Alistair had already joined a group that were off to the casino along with Jimmy. Renee, not wanting to third wheel, announced she would go and find Jenny and shot off with a cheeky wink at Alisha.

'Do you fancy grabbing fish and chips and sitting watching the tide go out?' Tom asked and she couldn't think of anything she wanted to do more. They found a restaurant aptly named Tom's Plaice and ordered open trays of crispy fish and chips, drowning in salt and vinegar. They perched on the wall, their feet dangling over the side and tucked into their dinners whilst trying to avoid the greedy gulls that had decided to land on the beach in front of them in the hopes of a discarded chip.

'It's been a lovely day,' she said to Tom as she threw the end of her fish to a particularly cheeky looking gull and wrapped her paper up tightly. Tom had already finished and took her wrapping off her, depositing it in a bin before heading back quickly.

'The tide has gone out enough now if you fancy a walk back to the hotel.' Alisha nodded, and he took her hand to help her up.

A steep set of stairs led to the beach, and Alisha took her shoes off. She'd always loved the feel of sand between her toes, Tom did the same and they just walked, side by side as the sun starting setting and the waves washed gently out to sea. Alisha's shoulders and arms felt a little stiff, probably from all the arcade games.

'Wow, we've walked miles.' She turned around and realised that The Bucket and Spade Hotel was way back in the distance and that where they were was nothing. Not a building, not a person, not even a noisy gull. 'We'd best walk back.'

'Alisha?' Tom touched her arm, and she turned back to him. He didn't say anything else; he didn't need to. She knew exactly what he wanted, and she wanted the same. There were no words needed to convey the feelings that she was having, and she knew from his pained expression that he felt exactly the same.

Both of them dropped their shoes and almost crashed into each other in their haste to be touching. Their arms wound around the other's back, snaking up to necks, hands delved into hair, mouths kissed mouths and tongues teased.

'I've missed you, Tom.' She ignored the pain that seeped through her body and put the sick feeling down to nerves. They crumpled onto the floor, her legs wrapping around him to pull him closer.

'I've missed you too.' His hands brushed her shoulders as he made to take off the boob tube, she was wearing, and she almost screamed out and couldn't hold back the flinch. 'Are you ok?'

Alisha pressed a finger gingerly to her shoulders; they were red hot.

'I think I've got sun burn.' She couldn't believe it. It was almost dusk, but there was enough light from a nearby lamp to allow her to see how red her arms were.

'Jesus, Alisha!' Tom looked at her back. 'Haven't you had sunscreen on? You're like a tomato.'

'I feel dizzy.' She wanted to throw up, the whole beach had started to spin, and she just wanted to lie there and not move. The damp sand felt glorious on her hot skin, but the gritty sand was rubbing, so she sat up. 'I want to throw up.'

'Let's get you back to the hotel.' He pulled out his phone. 'I'll call an Uber.' He tutted. 'Great, no signal.' He stood up and helped her to her feet gently. 'Just lean on me.' She did as she was told and felt like she was drunk. Every footstep seemed to jar into her shoulders and her stomach was swirling like a washing machine.

'I'm sorry, Tom.' She couldn't believe their night had ended this way.

'We've got plenty of nights ahead of us, don't you worry.' He sat her down on a bench as they reached civilisation again. 'There's a late-night chemist here, I'll go and get some painkillers and camomile lotion.'

Alisha rested her back against the cold window of the chemist and swallowed hard to stop herself from being sick. She closed her eyes; it was better that way.

'Hi, Alisha.' A male voice that wasn't Tom was speaking to her, and she begrudgingly opened her eyes. 'I'm Doctor Berry, can I just take your temperature?' She nodded slightly and wished she hadn't. 'Do you feel sick?'

'Ah ha.' She didn't dare move her head again.

'I'll grab my car and drive you to your hotel.' She heard Dr Berry say. 'She's got sunburn and heatstroke, I'm afraid. It's a good job I was here.'

The next thing Alisha knew was being tucked into bed by Tom and Dr Berry, and then she fell asleep.

Chapter 25

Alisha woke up in a room that was unfamiliar to her but to the smell and feel of someone who was completely and utterly familiar. She was dressed in pants and the boob tube she had been wearing yesterday. Tom was fast asleep, his hair falling onto his face, and she resisted the urge to brush it away in case she woke him up. He'd had a long night looking after her. She had no idea what time it was, but from the light filtering through the gaps in the curtains; she guessed it to be late morning at the very least.

She crept over to the dressing table and looked at herself in the mirror. She was covered in white blotches all over her shoulders, back, arms and chest, and Tom had even put some lotion on her nose and cheeks where that too had caught the sun. That would teach her to use old sunscreen and not buy a new one.

She winced when she tried to take the boob tube off and decided it was never coming off again. Her skin was now a bright pink, which was a vast improvement on the angry red she had seen last night in the streetlight.

'Good morning, beautiful.' Tom's voice from the bed made her look behind.

'Not covered in this stuff, I'm not.' She grimaced again as she tried once more to remove her top.

'Here, let me.' He crawled off the bed and she noticed he was only wearing boxer shorts and she couldn't help drinking in the sight of him. His body was nicely toned, slightly tanned, with just a small smattering of hair around his nipples and from his belly button, down into his shorts. 'Do you like what you see?' He was standing in front of her now, both eyebrows raised quizzically.

'Sorry.' She averted her gaze, but he shook his head and crooked a finger under her chin, turning her gaze back to him.

'Don't ever be sorry.' He reached down and kissed her, but, when he touched her shoulders, she sank down away from his touch. 'Let's see if we can get you out of these clothes and get you in the shower.'

'I don't think I can handle a shower.' The thought of the water beating down on her skin was too much. 'A nice cool bath sounds like bliss though.'

'Your wish is my command.' He kissed her softly and headed into the bathroom and as she heard the water running, there was a knock on the door.

'I'll get it.' She wrenched open the door to see a handsome man standing there dressed smartly in jeans and a shirt.

'I know I usually ask my patients to undress but it's rare they answer the door with their clothes already off.' He was smiling and Alisha blushed as she realised, she was still in the boob tube and her knickers. What on earth must this man think of her?

'I'm so sorry.' She grabbed the closest piece of clothing, which happened to be the sundress she had been planning to wear. She hitched it over her legs and onto her waist but didn't pull it up over her shoulders.

'Well I can see that you're definitely feeling much better than you were last night.' His voice sounded familiar.

'Dr Berry?' she said, as recognition dawned on her.

'Cran please.' He held out his hand. 'I told your husband I'd come and check on you today before I headed off to work.'

'Oh, he's not my husband.' She didn't know why she felt the need to say this so quickly, but she wasn't mistaken in the smile that flashed across his face.

'Boyfriend?' She shook her head at this as well and his smile grew bigger. 'I'll say goodbye then.' He held out his hand once more and she shook it, lingering a lot longer than was necessary or professional.

'Goodbye, Dr Berry, I mean Cran.' She corrected herself as Renee emerged in the hallway. 'And thank you again.'

She watched him walk down the stairs with a backward wave.

'Who was that hottie?' Renee stepped inside the room.

'Dr Berry, he came to check on me.' Alisha didn't know if Renee knew what had happened, but she assumed Tom would have at least told one of her family and if it was Alistair then the whole factory would know by now.

'I wish my doctor looked like him.' She sat down on the bed. 'Did he say his name was Cran?' Alisha nodded. 'Oh My God, Alisha!'

'What?' Alisha didn't know what Renee was getting so excited about a name for.

'His name is Cran Berry.' Alisha still didn't understand. 'Cranberry, like your dream.' Alisha's hand flew to her mouth. 'He's your future husband.'

'Who is whose future husband?' Tom had come in from the bathroom and was now dressed in jeans and a t-shirt.

'Oh one of the staff got engaged last night.' Renee covered quickly. 'Well, I'll be going. Are you coming to the fair later?'

Alisha nodded. 'I wouldn't miss it for the world.'

'We'll see you there then.' She waved and made a hurried exit and Alisha knew the WhatsApp group was about to blow up.

'Shall we get you undressed then?' Tom asked, and it was the most unsexy moment of her life.

As predicted, the WhatsApp group chat went crazy when Renee posted about Dr Cran Berry and both Lizzie and Fay wanted to know all the details. She promised to fill them in later and then put her phone on silent and enjoyed the cool water of the bath that Tom had run for her. He helped her to take her top off, which was awkward and painful, but then made a tactful exit and left her to bathe on her own.

Her thoughts whirled around her head. The traveller woman had said the cranberry in her dreams was a name, but surely it wasn't that obvious? And if it was, what was she meant to do with that information now she'd met him. Dump Tom and declare undying love to Dr Berry? No, it was just a dream, and that was that.

'Are you ok getting out?' Tom called gently from the door.

'I'll be fine, thanks; you don't need to hang around and wait for me if you don't want to.' She wrapped a towel around her body, being careful not to touch the sore bits and then patted herself dry. 'You looked after me enough last night.'

'But I thought everyone was going to the fair?' The door to the bathroom opened, and he stood there, a look of hurt on his face. 'Don't you want to go with me?'

'Of course I do.' This was the truth. 'I just thought you might want to spend some time with the Walker lot.'

He came up behind her, threaded his arms around her waist, and managed to somehow miss every single part of her that was sore. 'I see enough of them at work.' He kissed her cheek. 'Now, let's get you covered in some after sun lotion, and I hope you've got a long sleeve top in your case.'

Everyone had been instructed to meet by the big wheel on the pier, and Alisha was overjoyed to see that it looked like nearly everyone had. Even Juliet had joined them and had already challenged her children to a race on the Donkey Derby game. This was something they'd all enjoyed playing when they visited the local theme park as kids. They'd loiter around at the end of the day, waiting for a spot where it would just be the five of them playing.

Their dad would hand over five pounds to the attendant and then they would all grab their balls and start rolling them towards the various holes, yellow for one move, red for two moves and then the centre blue for three moves. They would scream and shout, accuse each other of cheating and then cheers when one of them was declared the winner.

'Come on then, you rabble.' Juliet paid the attendant and the four of them sat down on the stools, no one else daring to join them.

'Three, two, one, go!' The attendant shouted, and the staff cheered as the four Joneses rolled ball after ball, watching their donkey move along the course, cheering when they scored more than one move and sighing when they missed. In the end, it was Alistair that was triumphant, and he chose a cuddly Mickey Mouse to take home to Daniel.

'Round two?' Alistair looked at his family.

'I'm game if you are?' Alison sat back down on the seat, followed by Alisha and Juliet, this time Tom, Renee, and Jimmy joined in too.

The attendant started the race once more and yet again, Alistair won.

'I am the champion!' he roared, handing in his small Mickey for the next size up.

'Wait a minute.' Alisha looked over at Tom. 'You cheated; you've got three balls!' Sure enough, in the pit of Alistair's space were three red balls when everyone else only had two.

'You little shit!' Alisha and Alison raced after him as he'd already shot off with his prize, teasing and laughing at them.

'One last go?' Alistair asked as the three of them arrived back at the game, puffing and panting. Alisha and Alison nodded.

Tom ensured everyone only had two balls this time and as the attendant called go, the four of them furiously rolled the balls as quickly as they could.

'Winner, winner, chicken dinner!' Alisha cheered as her donkey rang the bell first to signal the end of the race, with Alison's just one step behind. In the end, she gave the toy to Alistair to give to Danny and he handed them all back to get the big dinosaur for him instead.

'Now for some rides.' Alistair rubbed his hands together and everyone departed in various directions, leaving Tom and Alisha alone.

'Fancy the big wheel?' he asked, but she shook her head. 'Log flume?' Another shake of the head. 'Go-karts?'

'Go on then.' She started to walk slowly, reluctantly, then suddenly ran off shouting at him. 'Last one there buys dinner.'

'You little tease.' Tom sped after her. 'Alisha look out!' But Alisha hadn't heard, she'd been too busy running and looking behind her to see where Tom was that she hadn't noticed the ice cream sign and went tumbling headfirst over it, spreading her hands out in front of her to stop her scraping her face.

'Ouch.' She wasn't sure if it was her body or pride that was more hurt by the fall.

'Alisha, are you ok?' Tom was kneeling on the floor next to her within seconds. 'You really are in the wars this weekend, aren't you?' He helped her up. 'Let's get you to the first aid station, I think it was by the entrance.'

She hobbled off on Tom's arm, her ankle felt like it was swelling, she had gravel stuck in the cuts on her hands and her shoulder felt sore on top of the sunburn.

There was a small queue at the first aid office, just two families with children looking much the same as Alisha, and after the nurse had shown these in and then out again, it was now her turn.

'Next please.' The nurse stood by the open door and ushered Alisha inside.

'What seems to be the trouble?' The doctor looked up from his desk. 'Well, I wasn't expecting to see you again so soon.'

Chapter 26

'Hello, Doctor Berry.' Alisha sat down on the chair, and he gave her a funny look. 'I mean Cran.'

'What have you done now?' He stepped out from behind the desk and for the first time she noticed how broad his shoulders were, he definitely worked out or exercised regularly at the very least she thought to herself and then shook her head. 'Cut hands, something going on with the shoulder from the looks of your top, anything else?' She was amazed at how quickly he had made his examination and assumed this was a doctor thing.

'I think I've sprained my ankle as well.' He knelt down in front of her and took hold of her ankle. She was only wearing sandals and she could feel the warmth from his hands on her skin.

'Yep, it's starting to swell, so we'll need ice on that as soon as possible.' He stood back up and called to someone to fetch him an ice pack and some crutches. He then walked over to a cupboard and pulled out various things, placing them on a metal trolley. Alisha found herself fascinated as she watched him. He had decent sized hands; long fingers and she was surprisingly pleased to see that he wasn't wearing a wedding ring. *And why should that matter?* 'Let's get you cleaned up, shall we, and then check your shoulder.'

'Thank you.' She hadn't realised he was now sitting in front of her and had taken hold of one of her hands.

'It might sting a bit.' Alisha had never found a trip to the doctor's to be erotic before, but then she'd never had a doctor that looked even remotely like Dr Berry before. As he picked the gravel out of her skin and bathed the wounds with antiseptic, she found herself strangely turned on. 'All done, just need to check the shoulder.' She hadn't noticed that he had finished and was still holding her hands out. 'I'll need you to take your top off if you can.'

'I'll try.' She resisted the urge to say something saucy, after all, he was being totally professional it was only her mind that was being dirty. 'I haven't got a bra on.' She didn't know why she said that she wouldn't have said it if the doctor had been female or if, in fact, it had been anyone other than this handsome specimen that stood before her. She hadn't been able to cope with the pain that the straps were causing on her sore skin, so she had dispensed with it, thankful that the top she had on had support built in.

'Do you want me to fetch the nurse in if you don't feel comfortable?' She shook her head. 'Just pop behind the screen for me please and let me know when you're ready.'

She felt so embarrassed by what she'd just said, what did it matter to him whether she had a bra on or not, he was a doctor, he must have seen hundreds of boobs in his life. Just because she was having thoughts about his hands didn't mean he was having them about her and anyway, wasn't she with Tom?

But was she with Tom? They weren't even boyfriend and girlfriend. How could she call him her boyfriend if he was married to someone else, whether it was just a technicality or not. In the eyes of the world, he was married and that was that. How could they go on dates? Was she to be his bit on the side, after all? Meeting in dark corners, snatched kisses and creeping home in the dark. Was this what she wanted?

'I'm ready.' She called from behind the screen. Now then, did she just sit there with her boobs on show, cover them with her hands? In the end, she held her top over her chest and turned the injured shoulder towards the screen.

'Well I can see straight away you've grazed most of your shoulder and back on your left side and your sunburn is a lovely bright pink.' She heard him wheel the trolley in. 'A bit more stinging, I'm afraid.'

By the time Cran had cleaned her wounds and she was back outside the screen, there was a pair of crutches leaning on the desk and an ice pack.

'Thank you,' she said as he handed her the ice pack after he'd shown her how to use the crutches.

'Will you be ok getting back to the hotel?' She nodded. 'I'm afraid it's rest for you for a few days until that ankle goes down and I'd suggest getting some paracetamol and ibuprofen for the pain and to help with the inflammation.' She hobbled towards the door, the crutches making her feel awkward. 'Are you sure you're ok? I'm on break in an hour, I could drive you back then.'

'Tom's outside.' Did she imagine the look of disappointment on his face? 'We'll get an Uber.'

'That's a good idea.' He walked towards the door but hovered over the handle. 'I don't usually do this,' he said, his eyes on the floor and his feet shuffling nervously. 'But I'd like to take you to dinner one day if that would be ok?' He didn't allow her to answer. 'No, of course that won't be ok, you've clearly got a someone and obviously don't live round here and I'm your doctor so forget I said anything.' He stepped away from the door and back to his desk without looking at her.

Feeling daring, Alisha turned to him. 'Perhaps I could take your number?' He looked up at her, his blue eyes dancing. 'You know, just in case I should need you for something?' He smiled and quickly wrote on a prescription note.

'You take care now.' He opened the door, and she hobbled out, Tom by her side in an instant. 'And call me if you need anything, anything at all.'

'I will.' Tom took the ice pack out of her hands and went to take the prescription, but she somehow managed to shove it in her pocket. 'It's only for painkillers, it will be cheaper to just buy them over the counter, you know what doctors are like.'

'I'm sorry, the weekend has been a washout.' Tom was helping her pack on the Monday morning. 'You didn't have to stay with me, you know.'

'But I wanted to.' He smiled at her. 'We still had fun, didn't we?'

She nodded. They had had fun. They'd ordered pizza and eaten it in bed watching Rom Coms and then binge watched the entire first season of The Summer I Turned Pretty to which Alisha declared she was now obsessed with and was one hundred percent Team Jeremiah. She'd fallen asleep just as Tom had been about to start season two and when she woke in the night, it was to find him curled up behind her, her back resting against his chest and his hand on her hip. It didn't feel how it had felt before though. When they'd last shared a bed back in May for those glorious few days, it had been loving and sensual, but she just couldn't get over the feeling that it was wrong, no not wrong, tainted. She still fancied him and when she looked at him, she wanted nothing more than to kiss him, but her brain kept repeating over and over that he was married and she just couldn't get past that, no matter how many times she told herself it wasn't real.

'I've enjoyed it.' He must have sensed something in her tone.

'But?' He came and sat down on the bed next to her.

'But I don't think I can get past it Tom.' There, she'd said it. 'I know you keep saying it's in name only, but you're still married, you married someone else whilst apparently in love with me.

'I really messed up, didn't I?' she nodded. 'Can we at least be friends?'

'Of course,' she replied, but she knew, outside of work, she wouldn't see him. 'I hope you and Katie will be happy together.'

'We're still going through with the annulment.' He took hold of her hands. 'Yes, you were a factor in it, but ultimately we both realised that we were only doing it for our parents and that wasn't a good enough reason, in fact it's not any reason to marry someone.'

'You're a good man, Tom.' She placed a hand on his cheek, and he leant into it. 'And one day you'll find the right woman.'

'What if I already have?' He turned his head and placed a kiss in her palm. 'It's ok, I understand. I'm not asking you to do anything you don't feel comfortable or happy with.' He stood up and went back to their packing. 'Just promise me one thing. If you ever change your mind, you'll call me.' He had both their bags and was now by the door. 'I'll get Alistair to come and help you down.'

'I won't change my mind, Tom.' She was adamant about this. 'Please don't wait for me.'

'I'd wait until the end of time for you Alisha.' And then he was gone, out of the door and she couldn't follow. When she was finally on the coach, she realised he was on the other one and when Renee pressed her as to what had happened, she broke into tears.

Chapter 27

By the end of October, Christmas was in full swing at the factory. Production had been ramped up, overtime was a regular occurrence and whilst most people were out grabbing pumpkins and Halloween decorations, Alisha was chatting baubles and tinsel with her family.

She'd been exchanging messages with Cran since the bank holiday and they'd been trying to arrange a weekend to meet up but so far they'd been unsuccessful in finding one when they were both free but with the summer season coming to an end, Cran would soon be finished with his work at the theme park and she was currently smiling at a rather saucy message he had just sent her involving exactly what he'd like to do with his stethoscope.

'We've got to get that order out.' Uncle John was in a bit of a panic, and it instantly brought her out of her daydream. 'I don't understand what went wrong.'

'These bloody new systems that's what.' Alistair was almost ripping his hair out. 'There's never been an issue before but now the stock levels aren't right which means we haven't ordered the stuff in. It's just a nightmare, Uncle John.'

'Where's Marsha?' Juliet looked around the room.

'She's over with Mr Walker and Tom, seems they're having a similar issue.' Alison said and Alisha purposefully didn't look up at his name. They hadn't really seen each other these past two months, just now and again at work. Tom had almost instantly reverted back to working at Walkers, and Marsha had somehow become the go between for the two companies.

'Well bloody well get her back here,' Juliet insisted. 'These are her bloody systems so she can bloody sort them.' She threw her hands up in the air. 'Honestly, it's like the bloody payroll all over again and we never got to the bottom of that one.'

Alisha pondered on her mum's comment for a while, then stood up and announced her intention to visit Dunnings.

'Why on earth do you want to go there?' Alistair asked.

'I've just got a feeling about something.' She grabbed her bag and laptop and headed off to the car park, got in her car and drove to the other side of town where the Dunnings premises were. It was very grey in comparison to Frosts. But then, with all the glitter and lights, she supposed most things would look grey in comparison.

'What on earth are you doing here?' Lizzie had come down to meet her after receiving a text.

'I need to see Mr Dunning, Senior.' Alisha added the senior as an afterthought. 'Is he in?'

'He is, but what's this all about?' Lizzie seemed curious.

'I can't say at the moment, wish I could, but if I'm right, then many things will be falling into place.' Lizzie looked at her and shrugged.

'Well then, have a seat and I'll see if he's free.' Lizzie disappeared through the door she had come through and Alisha sat down in one of the chairs.

She couldn't believe she hadn't put this connection together before, it was so blindingly obvious now she thought about it. She just needed her suspicions confirmed by Mr Dunning Senior and then she would need another look at the payroll files before she could tell the police. If it was as she suspected, it was definitely a police matter.

Alisha's meeting with Mr Dunning Senior had gone immensely well and her initial suspicions had been confirmed, all she needed to do now was to find the proof so she could take it all to the police.

'Are you coming, Alisha?' Alison asked as she packed her bag up at the end of the day. Everyone else had already left the office, although there were still people on the factory floor as there would be till around ten o' clock that evening.

'I'm just going to stay and work a bit longer on this,' Alisha said, not taking her eyes off the screen.

'Will you tell me what exactly it is that you think you've found?' Alisha shook her head. 'Will you tell us when you've found it?'

'Of course.' Alisha nodded. 'I just can't risk anything being said.'

'Ok then.' Alison walked over to the door. 'Just make sure you eat something and don't be here on your own. It's

Halloween, so there will be lots of people about and not everyone will be after sweets.'

Alisha knew Alison was referring to last year when a group of people had seen the lights on in the factory and decided to just walk in off the street.

'I won't,' Alisha agreed.

'And don't forget we're taking Grandma and Grandpa out on Saturday for their anniversary.' Alisha really didn't need reminding of this, Grandpa Frost was now at a stage where he was well enough to go out and about again. He'd been home for just over a month and although his mind wandered sometimes, and he would often get confused, he hadn't got any worse and the tablets seemed to have stabilised his condition.

With her mind totally focused on the screen, she didn't notice how fast the time was going. She had her pods in, so she didn't hear the machines switching off or the evening shift calling goodnight to each other as they walked out. Didn't hear the cars driving away or the last worker locking the factory shutters. It was only when the printer ran out of paper that she stood up and realised that it was almost midnight.

'Oh fuck it to damnation.' Although she didn't mind being in the factory on her own, she didn't like it at night, and she especially didn't like it at almost midnight on Halloween. She put her pods away in their case, saved her work and switched off her computer, but as she went to grab her coat and bag, she heard a noise. 'What the fuck was that?' she asked out loud, all the ghost stories she'd heard as a kid coming back into her head and making her see and hear things.

She opened the door of her office and looked onto the landing and down the stairs. It was in complete darkness and the light switches were located at the bottom of the stairs to be switched on when you came in and when you left. Either Alison had turned them off being on automatic pilot or the shift supervisor had, thinking they'd been left on by accident.

Pulling out her phone, she clicked on the torch and then turned her office light off and shut the door. Although the light was bright, it was causing shadows to form in the corners, and this was causing her brain to go into overdrive and imagine all sorts of things. Then suddenly it went off altogether and her phone died.

'Fucking hell.' She had started down the stairs and was now in complete darkness, but she could see a light coming up towards her.

'Alisha.' *Was that Tom's voice?* 'Alisha, are you here?'

'Tom?' she called back. 'Tom, where are you?'

'I'm here.' His voice startled her by its nearness, and she sensed that he was in front of her. 'I'm always here.'

The last three words were almost a whisper, but she heard them. 'My phone just bloody died on me.'

'Well mine isn't the best, but it should be enough to get us back down safely.' She linked her arm through his and together they made their way slowly down the stairs and out into the dark car park. The streetlights had already switched off as it was now after midnight, and it was pitch black except for the tiny light on Tom's phone.

'How did you know I was here?' she asked as he continued to shine the light so she could lock up, making a mental note to have a word with the supervisor, who clearly hadn't checked that the office was secure for the night.

'I saw the light on when I drove past and then saw your car in the car park.' She had to forcibly stop herself from asking where he'd been or where he was going, it was of no concern of hers what Tom Walker was up to.

'Here's my car.' Having been one of the first to arrive that morning, her car was right by the factory. 'Thank you for coming to rescue me. I'm not sure how I would have made it down the stairs otherwise. I kept seeing all sorts of shadows and hearing all kinds of noises, that'll teach me to watch horror films and then work late.' She was aware that she was babbling. It had been weeks since she had seen him and despite sexy texts and phone calls with Cran, her mind would still wander off to Tom and despite herself, she knew she was still in love with him.

'I've missed you, Alisha.' He had somehow taken hold of her hand without her realising, and the electricity that was coursing through her veins at his touch was intense. How she'd missed him, his voice, his smell, his touch.

Whether it was the darkness or just her heightened senses due to the past few minutes, but every nerve end was tingling.

'I've missed you too, Tom.' She placed a hand on to his cheek, wishing she could see his face clearly, but she knew it would be sad. 'But…'

'You're with someone else, aren't you?' His voice was barely a whisper, as if he didn't say it, it wouldn't be true. 'It's that doctor, isn't it?' Had her interactions with Cran been that obvious? 'I saw how he looked at you.'

'It's not that.' This was the truth, but she should have phrased it differently.

'So you are seeing him then?' he said, and she didn't know how to answer. She wasn't seeing him as such, they'd exchanged texts and spoken on the phone and there had been one instance where she was a little drunk and had Facetimed him and they'd had phone sex but seeing him was a big stretch of the imagination to say the least.

'I'm not seeing anyone,' she replied. 'I just can't Tom, I want to, I really, really want to, but every time I think I'm over it, I remember seeing you and Katie outside the castle. You looked so happy, the pair of you. You make a lovely couple.'

'I didn't know you'd seen us.' This was the first time she'd told anyone what she'd seen that day. 'It was all an act Alisha, how many times do I need to tell you?'

'A hundred, a thousand, I don't know. I don't know if it will ever make a difference either way.' She reached up and placed a soft kiss on his lips. 'Perhaps we just weren't meant to be.'

'I don't believe that Alisha, not for a second.' He went to walk away, but then turned straight back and kissed her. Her back was up against her car, and she felt his hands on her waist, his mouth almost rough in its passion. His hands moved up her neck and into her hair, hers doing the same, matching him kiss for kiss. Then almost as soon as it had started, he stopped. 'There is no way two people can feel what we feel for each other, to have the chemistry that we have and not be meant to be together.' He spoke breathlessly. 'I love you, Alisha.' And without waiting for her to answer, he headed off into the darkness.

Chapter 28

'Will you stop moping over Tom and give Dr Berry a call and arrange to meet up with him?' It was almost the end of November and Alisha was out with the girls before December and the Christmas season arrived in full swing. She'd given all her information to the police and was just waiting to hear from them as to what they planned to do. 'He is the man you're going to marry, after all.'

'Why don't you go down and surprise him this weekend?' Lizzie suggested. 'You know where he lives don't you.' She nodded. He'd sent her a bunch of flowers in the post to the factory for her birthday and there was a return address on the back, so she'd popped the information into her phone to be possibly used at a later date.

'I can't just turn up on his doorstep,' Alisha insisted.

'And why not?' Fay asked. 'He obviously put his address for a reason, he didn't have to you know.'

So, two days later, she found herself driving to Somerset and checking in at The Bucket and Spade. Jamie was surprised but delighted to see her and offered her his best room. As it was November, there weren't very many people there, so it was wonderfully quiet. After she'd unpacked, she headed into the town centre and grabbed a gingerbread latte before sitting on the rocks, looking out to sea.

It was cold, and the sea was rough, the odd splash hitting her face as the waves broke against the rocks, but she was wrapped up in her favourite coat with the Christmas tree scarf her grandma had knitted for her a few years ago. She loved winter, always had. Cosy nights in front of the fire reading, hot chocolate in bed and fluffy pyjamas.

With the warmth of the latte inside, she popped Cran's postcode into her phone and realised that he was only a ten-minute walk away, so she threw her cup in the bin, pulled every ounce of courage to her feet, and followed Siri as she told her which way to go.

As she turned onto his road, her courage deserted her, and she came to a dead halt. She really couldn't just turn up on his doorstep, could she? In the end, the decision was taken out of her hands as about halfway down the street she saw Cran walk out of a house and on to the pavement, stopping to wait. There was a young girl of around five holding his hand. Then a few seconds later a dark-haired woman came out of the same house with a dog on a lead.

Alisha knew instantly that they were a family. There was something about the way he looked at her and she at him that made them a couple, even before she took hold of his hand. Alisha should have been upset; she should have been raging but was relieved to find she felt absolutely nothing. Then when she realised they were heading her way, she darted off around the corner and back to the hotel.

Back in her room and Alisha found herself smiling, the smile turned into a giggle and then the giggle into a full belly laugh. She rolled on her bed, tears streaming down her face at the relief that washed over her. Relief at what though? Relief that she didn't have to try and pretend something with Cran because of some silly dream? Yes, he was attractive, and she'd certainly enjoyed the moments they'd shared, but it wasn't real, they'd not shared dates or even a kiss so it had all been just an enjoyable fantasy. A distraction.

And she knew exactly what the distraction was from. Tom. She hadn't stopped thinking about him since their kiss on Halloween. She'd agonised over her decision to cut him out of her life over and over again when all he was doing was trying to protect his family. Wouldn't she have done the same? Marrying someone was perhaps a little on the extreme side, but there weren't many things she wouldn't do.

With her decision made, she wasted no time. She packed all her things, apologised to Jamie that she wouldn't be needing the room anymore, paid in full anyway even when he insisted that she didn't need to and then got in her car and drove to Tom's house.

It was only when she was around five minutes from Walkers that she remembered she didn't actually know where Tom lived and only had the vague knowledge of the street, she'd dropped him off at.

Luckily she had a good memory and headed there in the hope that if she drove around for a bit, she might spot his car or even better, him or his parents because she knew he still lived at home, she didn't allow the thought that he'd moved in with Katie to surface in her head and pushed it away instantly before it got any traction and derailed her. She trusted Tom, trusted that he was telling the truth. He had no feelings for Katie other than friendship. He'd married her purely to save his and her family names, nothing else.

She drove round a few of the streets, her body was aching from the two-hour drive and the earlier two-hour drive, but she was determined to find him. As she got further away, the houses became less opulent, and she was positive she must have gone too far. But then, just as she passed by a row of shops, she was sure she had seen Mr and Mrs Walker with a small terrier type dog on a lead.

After a quick U turn, she was back by the shops and saw the couple again. It was unmistakably them and Alisha was a little shocked to see how normal they looked, not that they hadn't looked normal before, but here they were dressed in jeans with mud splattered boots and were walking arm and arm along the pavement. Alisha didn't know why she had the impression they were posh, perhaps it was the aura Mary Walker had given off on that day at the factory.

They turned down one of the streets and Alisha was relieved to see it was a cul-de-sac, so she parked up quickly and followed them as closely as she dared. They walked down the short drive of number twenty and had Mr Walker not pulled out a key, Alisha would not have believed it was their house. It wasn't small, not by any stretch of the imagination, but it certainly wasn't the large mansion type houses Tom had insinuated that they lived in.

Now she was here, she didn't have a clue what to do. Tom's car was nowhere to be seen, and she didn't really want to knock on his parent's door, so she turned and made as swift of an exit as possible.

'Alisha?' She turned back at her name.

'Hello, Mr Walker.' Tom's dad was standing at the end of his drive.

'I thought it was you.' She knew she was going to have to explain her presence.

'I was just wondering if Tom was in?' They didn't need to know that she'd basically stalked them.

'Come on in and have a cup of tea, Mary will have the kettle on by now.' He tried to usher her towards him. 'We've just been out with the dog, but I've forgotten my paper, so I was just heading back to the shops.'

'I don't want to impose.' She really didn't. 'If Tom's not here, then I'll message him.' She probably should have just messaged him in the first place but surprising him had seemed such a good idea at the time.

'You're not imposing in the slightest.' He's hands were outstretched in welcome, but still she hesitated. 'It's Tom we'd like to talk to you about.'

Oh dear, she thought, they want to give me a good talking to about the whole debacle. 'If you're sure Mrs Walker won't mind.' She stepped towards him.

'Mrs Walker won't mind one bit.' He followed her down the drive and closed the door behind them as they stepped inside. 'Mary, we have a visitor.' The house was warm and welcoming. Photos of Tom lined the wall and there seemed to be a picture of him for every year he'd been alive.

The little terrier dog came bounding towards her and jumped up her legs.

'Don't mind Jess.' Mrs Walker came in from the kitchen. 'It's lovely to see you Alisha, come on through to the kitchen, the tea is just mashing.'

Alisha did as she was asked and walked into the beautifully light and spacious kitchen, there were even more photos of Tom, artwork from school pinned to the fridge and it was clear he was the apple of their eye. She sat down at the table and after some hustling and bustling and a few minutes of polite conversation, Mrs Walker turned to Alisha.

'Now, Mary.' Mr Walker's voice was soft, but Alisha could detect an almost warning tone. 'We promised him.'

'I don't care what we promised him, Bill.' Mrs Walker looked on the verge of tears. 'He's absolutely miserable without her and she needs to know.' Mary Walker turned to Alisha and took her hands in her own. 'Now Alisha, do you love my son?'

Alisha had to stop her mouth from dropping open, she hadn't expected this question at all and certainly not to open the conversation with.

'Mary!' Mr Walker's tone was almost scolding. 'That's none of our business.'

'It is when our son has disappeared off the face of the earth.' Alisha was in shock.

'Tom's gone?' Mr Walker shook his head.

'Mary has a tendency to over-exaggerate.' He gave his wife a look. 'He packed his bags a few weeks ago and said he needed to get away for a bit. We get the odd message to say he's ok, and that's it.'

'He is not OK, Bill,' Mary insisted. 'When will you see that?'

'What's happened?' Alisha asked.

'We were hoping you could tell us.' Bill and Mary were both looking at her now with such hope in their eyes. 'He came home late on Halloween, so very late, it was so unlike him. Then the next morning he packed a case and told us he was going away for a bit.'

'He's taken everything so personally,' Bill explained. 'It's my fault we lost the house not his. It's my fault we had to sell the business. He's such a good son and I let him forfeit his own happiness when I should have just swallowed my pride and stopped that blasted wedding from happening.'

'He told me he was happy to do it,' Alisha said, but Mary and Bill both shook their heads furiously.

'Neither of them were happy, they hated the lies, but Katie's solution about the quick annulment seemed to solve everything.' Mary suddenly burst into tears. 'The look on his face Alisha when he said his vows, it broke my heart.'

'What can I do to help?' Alisha didn't know what to make of it all.

'We just need to know if you love him?' Mary asked again. 'And if you do, could you forgive him?'

'Could you forgive us?' Bill asked.

'That's why I came here,' Alisha stated. 'I realised that perhaps I was a little harsh and maybe we could build something.'

'Oh, Alisha.' Mary stood up and threw her arms around her. 'You don't know how happy that makes us feel.'

Twenty minutes later when Alisha walked out of their house and back towards her car, she was still reeling from their conversation. There hadn't been anything massively shocking revealed except for the fact that they'd lost their house but knowing how upset Tom had been on the day and how he'd basically ran away after their kiss had just cemented in her brain that she'd treated him way too harshly and punished him long enough.

As soon as she was in the car, she picked her phone up, unplugged it from the Sat Nav and went to ring him. It was then she noticed a text from her sister.

Come quick. Alistair has been arrested for defrauding the company.

Chapter 29

The next week was a blur. What should have been the start of the Christmas season at Frosts, became a series of police investigations. The factory had to be closed because all the work computers had been taken away.

'But why are they being so over the top?' Alison had asked Juliet as they'd watched the police bag up and mark things for evidence. 'And why do they think Alistair is involved?'

'I don't know my lovely, but I know that none of my children would do this.' Alisha had squeezed her mum and sister's hands. 'I'm just glad your grandpa can't see it.'

Lizzie informed them that the police had also been to Dunnings, and they soon discovered that the Walker factory had also received a visit.

'Where the hell is Marsha?' Juliet asked the following Saturday morning. All the staff were in, everything had been returned and they were now a week behind with orders and it was going to be twenty-four-hour shifts from now until Christmas week at least. 'She's not answering my calls or messages, five times I've rung her.'

'Calm down,' John soothed. 'We're Frosts, we can do this.'

'Frosts never give up,' Alisha said.

'No, they bloody don't.' They all turned to see Alistair standing in the doorway.

'Alistair.' Alisha was the first to reach him. 'What are you doing here?'

'I've been released without charge.' He had lost weight in the week he'd been gone. 'They're charging Marsha with fraud. Turns out she's wanted all over the country for similar things and you'll never guess who her accomplish is…Jason.'

'I can't believe it.' John sat down in one of the chairs with a slump. 'But she's been so helpful, so good with Dad and setting up the new systems.'

'Exactly,' Alistair stated. 'That's what they do. They go around the country finding small family firms that need modernising and integrate themselves in, sometimes its Jason who does it and sometimes its Marsha. That isn't even their real names apparently.'

'How long has it been going on?' Alisha asked, looking at her family, all of them with a look of shock on their faces.

'Years and years,' he continued. 'They've got a proper little system. One of them starts a relationship with someone high up in the company if they can, wheedles themselves into a job and then brings in the idea of new software. This software then places glitches into the system to take sick pay, paternity pay, benefits in kind, you name it, this system did it and because it wasn't company money that was being stolen, it didn't seem to ever get picked up. They only usually do it for a year, two at the most the police said and then they move on, and the company ends up with a tax investigation.'

'What happened at Dunnings then?' Juliet asked. 'How did she get that glowing reference?'

'I can answer that,' Alisha piped up. 'Mr Dunning just wanted rid of her for shall we say personal reasons, so she agreed to go as long as he gave her the reference and then she just walked right into this place.' She put her hand to her mouth. 'Oh God! That's why Jason was with me wasn't it?'

'You and me both Alisha.' Alistair placed a hand on her shoulder, and she gave him a withering look. 'Sorry.' He apologised, she may have forgiven him, but it still hurt, and she had no desire to be reminded of it.

'I was the one that told her about Frosts in the first place.' Juliet looked horrified at this.

'We've all been taken for fools.' Alisha looked at her uncle, he seemed the most affected by it. 'I gave her the job, I let her in.'

'You weren't to know Uncle John,' Alison put her arm around him. 'We were all taken in by her. She even managed to worm her way into Alisha's affections in the end.'

'Affections is a little strong,' Alisha said. 'I tolerated her.'

'Well, I'm just glad that we can start getting back to some semblance of normality.' Juliet was standing by the door. 'Let's get this factory back up and running and make this our best Christmas ever.'

Her mum's enthusiasm for the factory and Christmas as a whole was still surprising to Alisha. For most of her life, she only ever remembered her mum hating the season and the factory and she'd never really understood why. It was only when they'd had a little heart to heart over lunch one day that she'd finally been able to work it out.

'I hated that your grandpa wouldn't let me work in the factory just because I wanted to have a family as well.' Juliet had explained. 'It's such an old-fashioned belief that women can't do both and we'd fully intended for your dad to stay home whilst I went to work but Dad still wouldn't have it. And then your dad got sick, so it wasn't even a possibility.'

'But why were you so down on Christmas as a whole?' Alisha could understand why her mum would be down on the factory but Christmas too.

'It just seemed easier that way,' her mum had shrugged. 'Then I did it for so long that it became part of me. Watching you kids start work in the factory was hard because I wanted nothing more than to do the same, to work alongside my brother and you three in the Frost family firm.'

'We should really rename it Jones you know,' Alisha had joked, and her mum smiled. 'There's far more of us now.'

This conversation had played over and over in Alisha's head for a while and her relationship with her mum had slipped into a more comfortable one, so much so that Alisha felt able to confide in her about Tom. Of course, she'd had multiple conversations on the subject with the girls, had even spoken with her sister about it, but she felt the need for an older woman's take on it.

'If you want something, Alisha,' her mum said. 'Then don't stop until you get it. Don't be like me, don't give up, don't allow anyone to tell you what you can and can't do. If you want to be with Tom, then you need to tell him.'

This was proving an extremely difficult task to achieve though. He wasn't answering her calls or texts and when she'd spoken with his parents, they informed her that all they got was a message once a day to inform them that he was just checking in.

'Hurry up.' The girls were at Alisha's house, like always getting ready for the Frost Christmas Ball. Alisha had gone all out this year and she couldn't wait to see everyone's faces. This was why she was being so impatient and insistent on them being early. 'I need to be there; I want to watch people arriving.'

'Take a chill pill, Lishe.' Lizzie was currently making her up do look messy by pulling the odd strand of hair here and there and then spraying half a can of hairspray.

'Jesus, you'll single handedly take out the ozone layer,' Fay complained.

'It's environmentally friendly I'll have you know,' Lizzie retorted. 'Alisha Jones, will you stop dancing around and just sit down and wait. We've got ages yet.'

Alisha knew she was right, but she'd been ready even before they arrived and was extremely tempted to go to the conference centre on her own, but she knew the girls would be disappointed, it was tradition that they always drove together in the limo.

There was more noise as Renee came back upstairs accompanied by Jimmy, David and Paul who were all suited and booted.

'The limo's arrived.' Alisha looked out of the bedroom window. 'Come on, Lizzie, how many more times can you move the same bit of hair around?'

'I'll have you know that it takes time to look this good.' She ran her hands down her body.

'You'd look good in a bin bag,' Paul said, stepping towards her and kissing her.

'Now I've got to redo my lipstick.' Alisha screamed in frustration. 'Ok, I'll do it in the car. Jesus, when did you get so tightly wound?'

Alisha almost shoved them all out of the house and into the car in her haste to be on the way and once the limo had taken off, she started to relax. The drive was filled with laughter and drinks and by the time they arrived, Alisha was feeling a little tipsy and a lot more like her old self.

'Fucking hell, Lishe!' The experience this year, started as soon as you turned into the drive. Fairy lights festooned the tree lined drive, boards had been put up to create a snowy scene and outside the hotel along with the usual giant Nutcrackers were eight reindeer, some elves and of course Santa. 'It's bloody wonderful.'

She could tell by their faces that it was good, their mouths were open in awe and their eyes wide in wonderment and she couldn't help feeling a sense of pride. It had been one hell of a year; things had happened that she would never have imagined. She'd found love and lost it, had even come to terms with it but her family and friends were there and always would be.

'Wait till you see inside.' Alisha didn't know whether she was more excited to see the whole thing come together for herself or for the guests. A carpet of fake snow led into the ballroom and somehow when you stepped inside, it was actually snowing.

'It's just like a snow globe,' Fay remarked, and this made Alisha smile because it was exactly what she had been hoping for. Other people were starting to arrive now, and Alisha's smile widened further at their reactions.

'You've done well.' She turned to find her mum and dad standing behind her. 'You're a right chip off the old block you are.' Juliet hugged her and then turned to her husband. 'I think you owe me a dance.'

'I think I owe you several.' He twirled her around and she giggled like a schoolgirl as they made their way towards the floor.

'I've never seen them so happy,' Alistair said. 'It's so lovely to see.' He placed an arm around Alisha's waist. 'I'm sorry for everything this year.' He rested his head on her shoulder. 'It's been one big fuck up.'

She leaned her head on top of his. 'Well, that's another thing we Frosts do well, fuck up big time.' They laughed. 'It all worked out in the end and that's what matters.'

'There's something else that might work out in the end too.' Alistair pointed towards the door and her heart stopped beating for just a second.

He was here, Tom was here.

She resisted the urge to run to him, after all, she had no idea how he would react but surely the fact that he was here, at the ball, meant there was hope. He hadn't seen her yet, but he seemed to be searching the room, then he turned behind him as his mother and father came in. Of course, he was here for them, for the company. Her heart sank and she turned away.

Chapter 30

'Why on earth are you hiding in here?' Renee scolded when she found Alisha skulking in the toilets. 'Get out there and ask him to dance.'

'He doesn't want me, Renee.' This was perfectly obvious to Alisha. 'If he wanted me, he'd have come and found me.'

'The fact that from almost the moment he arrived you've been in here, probably means that he hasn't been able to find you.' Renee yanked her up onto her feet. 'He's asked so many people where you are and when he asked me, I said I'd go and find you.' She looked Alisha up and down. 'No, this won't do at all.' She took Alisha's bag and fumbled around inside. 'Lips.' Alisha did as she was told and made the smile you only did when applying lipstick. Next, she took a piece of tissue. 'Blot.' Alisha pursed her lips together. 'Mascara's fine, cheeks ok, hair?' Renee seemed to be going through some mental checklist. 'Hair, good.' This was said after she'd fluffed and ruffled Alisha's hair. 'Boobs.' With this, she yanked Alisha's dress up and faffed with her cleavage. 'Perfect!' she declared.

'I'm glad I meet with your approval,' Alisha smirked.

'You always meet with my approval,' Renee squeezed her hand. 'Now, if you want him, go and get him.'

'Yes, Ma'am,' Alisha saluted and headed out of the door with a confidence she really didn't feel. Question after question raced through her head. What if he didn't want her? What if he'd changed his mind?

As she came out of the bathroom corridor and back into the ballroom, the party was well and truly in full swing. The back doors were open now and the fairground music was drifting inside, mixing with the disco. She scanned the room for him, her eyes searching quickly. Then they found him.

Whether it was coincidence or fate, but his gaze caught hers at the exact same moment and it was just like something out of the movies. Time seemed to stand still as she watched him walking towards her across the room. He was smiling at her, and she knew everything was going to be fine, she could tell, just from his face that he loved her still.

Then suddenly he was in front of her, standing there and she drank in the sight of him.

'Alisha.' Her name was like nectar on his lips. 'Alisha.' Wait, that wasn't Tom's voice. 'Alisha! Wake the fuck up, will you?'

'What, what's happening?' She opened her eyes to see the concerned face of Lizzie standing over her.

'We've been looking all over for you.' Alisha scanned the room and realised she was lying on a pile of clothes.

'Is this lost property or something?' she asked, picking up a decidedly smelly trainer and dumping it far away from her.

'What are you doing in here?' Lizzie helped her to her feet.

'I just needed to get away.' Alisha had wanted some space but everywhere she'd gone there had been someone there.

'Well you got away all right, the party's over and everyone's gone home.' Lizzie took out her phone and tapped a short message. 'At least they'll all know you're safe now. We've been worried sick.'

'Has Tom gone?' she asked, unsure what part of her dream had been real or not.

'Tom left ages ago. He brought his parents, stayed for about ten minutes, and left again.' Lizzie opened the door.

'Oh, thank God!' Fay and Renee were standing there. 'You gave us a good fright, missy.'

'We came to find you for the last dance and then we realised that none of us had seen you for hours.' Renee was clearly upset. 'We all thought something awful had happened to you.'

'I'm fine,' she hugged her friends. 'Just bummed I missed the party.'

'And Tom.' Lizzie reminded her.

'Forget men,' Alisha said. 'I've had enough of them. From now on it's me, myself, and I.' The three girls looked at her and then at themselves, a knowing look passing between them. 'I mean it. No more men.'

'Yeah, sure.' The four of them linked arms. 'Let's get home before the manager kicks us out.'

'I can't believe I missed the party,' Alisha said, pretending to be annoyed when really, she was annoyed at herself for missing yet another opportunity with Tom.

Christmas morning dawned, and Alisha stretched out in her bed and yawned. She felt chilled and relaxed and was again happy with her decision not to attend the traditional family gathering.

'But it won't be the same without you.' Juliet had said when she'd announced her decision. 'This is the first year we'll be altogether.'

'Mum, we're together every year and have been all my life.' Alisha had stated.

'You know what I mean. It's different this year,' her mum explained. 'It's been such a tough year for everyone.'

'And that's exactly why I just want a quiet Christmas at home on my own.' Her parents had finally understood that she just needed a few days of down time, space to just be herself for a while with no expectations on her.

She answered and sent numerous Merry Christmas messages before dragging herself out of bed and down the stairs to make herself blueberry pancakes. She curled up on the sofa and watched Home Alone and Santa Clause. Then she decided to start prepping for dinner.

It was the least stressful Christmas Day she'd ever had. She peeled a few vegetables, popped the tiny turkey crown in the oven and then opened a bottle of wine. She looked out of the kitchen window onto her back garden and realised that it had started snowing. It couldn't be a more perfect day.

By the time her dinner was ready, the snow was already a foot deep, and she'd managed to polish off almost a whole bottle of red, but she didn't feel drunk in the slightest. There was something about drinking alone that just made you feel a little bit melancholy.

She sat down at the table with her little dinner and had an immense feeling of de-ja-vu but didn't have a clue why. Reaching for the cranberry sauce she swore as she remembered she'd forgotten to buy it. She considered going without, but you really couldn't have Christmas dinner without cranberry sauce even though she didn't particularly like it, so she wrapped her dinner up in foil and popped it back in the oven.

Dragging on her boots, she trudged through the snow to the one and only shop that stayed open on Christmas Day. It was a good twenty-minute walk, but there were so many other people out walking dogs or walking off dinner that it passed in a flurry of hellos and Happy Christmas. She stomped off the snow as she went inside the store and headed straight for the condiments shelf.

There was a man already in the aisle. He was wrapped up in a big coat and bobble hat. Alisha swore loudly as she realised he was taking the last jar of cranberry sauce.

'Here, you can have it.' He turned and Alisha couldn't help smiling.

'Tom!' She almost skipped towards him. 'What are you doing here?'

'The same thing as you by the looks of it,' he handed her the jar. 'I'm not a huge fan anyway, just a kind of traditional thing isn't it.' He picked up a jar of mustard. 'I haven't even got a turkey; think I'll just have a beef sandwich or something.'

'Aren't you with your mum and dad?' He shook his head.

'Aren't you?' he asked.

'No.' Alisha couldn't believe he was here. 'I'm all peopled out this year.'

'Me too.' He looked sad, and she could tell he was reluctant to leave.

'Do you want to come and have dinner with me?' She watched indecision spread across his face. 'No pressure, no stress, just two people enjoying Christmas together.'

'I'd like that.' He put the jar of mustard down. 'I'd like that a lot.'

She nodded and headed for the till. 'You didn't walk all the way from your house, did you?'

'No, I've got the car, shall I meet you outside?' she smiled her answer. 'I'll see you in a minute then.'

Alisha couldn't believe it, here she was expecting to be alone on Christmas Day and now, well now she was going to be spending it with Tom.

'Don't fuck it up, don't fuck it up.'

'Excuse me?' The cashier asked and Alisha realised she'd been speaking out loud.

'Sorry,' she smiled nervously. 'Just this please.'

She felt like a teenager as they drove back to her house. The roads were getting quite treacherous now, and she was glad it was only a short drive, but part of her wanted to stay inside the confines of the car forever. There was an underlying tension between them, and it was causing Alisha to have very impure thoughts about Tom, especially when his hand brushed against her knee as he changed gear.

It had taken almost as long to drive back to her house as it had to walk, when Tom finally pulled up on her drive.

'Thank goodness for that.' He unclipped his seatbelt and leaned forward over the wheel to look up and out through the windscreen. 'It's really coming down, isn't it?'

'Tom?' His name was a question. She didn't have any idea what the question was, but she just knew that she had to ask it. He turned in his seat, one arm resting on the wheel, the other on his leg. 'Tom?' She asked again when he didn't answer.

He didn't speak, he just looked at her, his eyes seemed to be asking their own question. Neither of them spoke, they didn't have to. Words weren't needed, words had got them in trouble before, all that was needed now was actions.

Her hand found its way to his cheek, his hand was on her neck and together they crossed the gap, like an invisible force pulling them together until their lips touched, gently at first, like they were awaiting the other's permission and then with all the pent-up passion that they had been holding inside themselves.

It was Tom who broke away first. 'Shall we go inside?' He smiled at her.

She nodded. 'We probably should before we get snowed in.' It was only when they opened the car doors that they realised how much snow had fallen. 'I haven't seen this much snow since I was a kid.'

The snowflakes were continuing to fall thick and fast now and by the time they reached Alisha's front door they were covered. They shook themselves off in the hall.

'Dinner smells…er…good.' Tom hung his coat on the rack.

'Oh no!' There was a strong smell of burning coming from the kitchen and when she opened the oven door, smoke billowed out. 'It's ruined.' She threw it on the side in despair. 'I thought I'd put it on low.'

'It doesn't matter,' Tom said. 'We've still got the cranberry sauce.' He held up the jar and she started to laugh. 'Let's look in the cupboards and see what we can find.'

Half an hour later and they were sitting watching The Strictly Come Dancing Christmas Special and eating beans on toast.

'Some Christmas dinner, eh?' Alisha said.

'It's the best Christmas dinner I've ever had.' And she knew by the way that he said it and from the way that he was looking at her that he meant it. 'We really need to talk Alisha.'

She placed her plate on the floor and then moved over to him and he did the same. 'Let's talk tomorrow.' She was scared that if they talked one of them might say something that the other didn't like. 'Let's just have Christmas.' She climbed onto his lap and kissed him.

Chapter 31

Alisha dreamed the same cranberry dream again that night, only this time it wasn't a cranberry she was chasing but Tom. Each time she caught up to him he would run off again or disappear altogether until she tipped him out of the jar on Christmas Day but instead of turning into a wedding ring like the cranberry had on both occasions, Tom just sat on the side of her plate smiling up at her offering her a red heart in his hands.

That dream gets stranger and stranger, she said to herself, stretching out her legs and smiling when her foot encountered one of Tom's. It was such a wonderful feeling to wake up beside him again. He was asleep, his breathing deep and even, and she turned on her side to look at him. Whatever happened now, she was going to make damn sure that nothing was going to come between them again.

'Good morning, beautiful,' Tom said sleepily. 'I could get used to this.' He reached over and kissed her. 'I haven't slept so well in ages.' He gave her a cheeky grin, and she knew he was reminding her of last night and how they'd been so tired after making love no less than four times that they'd just fallen asleep in each other's arms. 'Fancy a repeat performance?'

She giggled as he dived under the duvet, and it was mid-afternoon before they ventured downstairs on the hunt for something to eat.

Alisha searched her fridge and cupboards and, as usual, they were virtually empty. 'We may need to go to the shop again,' she said, but Tom, who was currently looking out of the window, shook his head.

'Not unless you've got snowshoes and a sledge,' he said. 'It's a good couple of feet out there.' He came up behind her and looked in the cupboard himself. 'I could rustle us up some pancakes.'

'Pancakes sounds lovely.' She headed over to the kettle. 'I'll make us a coffee.'

'Tea for me, please,' he replied. 'I always have tea in the morning.'

'Oh yes, I should know that.' Something niggled in her head. 'Why did Marsha know that?' He looked at her blankly. 'That day, in the office when we were making drinks, she insinuated that she knew you drank tea in the morning. How would she know that?'

'Because she'd worked with us for a few weeks.' He was busy measuring flour onto the scales and his tongue stuck out the side as he concentrated.

'No one said. When was that?' Alisha was intrigued.

'A few years ago now, we sent her packing when she tried to come onto me and then Dad, would you believe it.' He was now breaking eggs.

'Oh trust me, I can believe it.' Alisha filled him in on everything he didn't know as they sat and ate the fluffy pancakes.

'It's been one hell of a year, hasn't it?' Tom said, pulling out his phone and showing her an email on it. 'I was going to print it off and bring it to you, but I didn't know if you would even open the door to me.' She didn't need to read it; she saw the court insignia and knew it was the official annulment of his marriage. 'I'm so sorry again, Alisha.'

Surprisingly, she was ok with it. 'It's over and done, it's in the past. All that matters now is how we move on from it.' She couldn't believe she was saying it, but she'd had enough of regrets and misunderstandings to last her a lifetime.

'I think being adopted just made me want to please my parents even more.' He took her hand. 'I'm so grateful to them for taking me in when I was a baby, they couldn't have loved me more if I was their blood. I've been given everything I've ever wanted, and I suppose I just wanted to do my best to help them, even if it cost me my own happiness.'

'You don't need to explain…wait…what did you say?' she looked at him. 'You're adopted?'

'Yep, I was orphaned at three months old, and my parents took me in from the church.' Alisha could see now why he'd wanted to repay his parents and the church to some extent for the kindness they'd shown him, and it explained a hell of a lot. 'My life could have been very different.'

'I've never met anyone that's been adopted before.' She wasn't sure why she said this, it just felt like she needed to say it. 'And I have to say, that I am very glad that your parents did adopt you because we might never have met.' She moved around to his side of the table and stepped over him, so she was astride him and facing him at the same time.

'We'd have found each other.' He kissed the tip of her nose. 'No matter what, we were meant to be together. From that first moment I saw you from across the fairground I knew you were the one for me.'

'Just a shame it took us so long.' She threw her arms around him and hugged him tight. 'To think that I almost let you walk out of my life,' she spoke into his neck, his stubble tickling her nose.

'I would never have done that, not until I'd exhausted every avenue.' He pushed her gently away from him so he could look earnestly into her face. 'I love you, Alisha Jones, with all my heart and soul, from our first Christmas to my last Christmas and all the Christmases in between.'

'I love you too, Tom Walker.' And she meant it, with every fibre of her being.

'You do know my name isn't Walker, don't you?' he asked, and she shook her head. 'Mum insisted on keeping my name as it was, so I never forgot my birth parents, but I've got Walker as my middle name.'

'So what's your real name then?' Alisha was curious.

'Thomas Walker Cranberry at your service.'

THE END

A Little Note

I can't quite believe that this is my tenth published novel and eleventh book counting my picture book.

Writing stories is an absolute dream come true for me and I'm looking forward to sharing the new ideas that I have whirling around my head at the moment.

This story began life a few years ago and sat in my laptop unfinished until the summer when I decided to complete my very first Christmas story.

A Cranberry for Christmas is inspired by one of my favourite Christmas songs, Christmas Wrappin' by The Waitresses and I thought it would make a great story. Alisha and Tom fall for each other instantly but it takes a whole year of hits and misses before they finally get their HEA.

Thanks as always to my family.

A special shout out to my Finham Park Crew, without them I would not be me.

To my friends in the wonderful world of social media, thank you for your continued love and support.

Thanks again to Kelly who edits my words and to Amanda who makes my covers into paperbacks.

Happy 100th birthday to my nannie for the 18th of October.

All that's left for me to say is Happy Christmas.

Love Charlie xx

About the Author

I was born in Coventry but now live in Nuneaton. I married the love of my life nearly 25 years ago and we have two grown-up children. We share our lives with two mad dogs as well.

Writing is a great passion of mine. I love creating stories and characters, they help me escape from the world for a while and I hope readers feel the same.

I am a huge fan of All Creatures Great and Small, Call the Midwife and Bridgerton. I love history and romance.

I also write under Florence Keeling and for children as Lily Mae Walters.

Coming Soon

Look out for my new releases next year.

Also by Charlie Dean

I Love You, Always, Forever

The Pumpkin Pact

By Florence Keeling

A Little in Love

The Word is Love

Please Remember Me

Love, Lies and Family Ties

By Lily Mae Walters

Josie James and The Teardrops of Summer

Josie James and The Velvet Knight

Brittle's Academy for The Magically Unstable

Follow me on X

@CharlieADean

@KeelingFlorence

@LilyMaeWalters1

Printed in Dunstable, United Kingdom